"The time of initiation is at hand."

They tied Skip's hands and feet to the crate. The cloth bag was ripped from his head. Suddenly a bright light flashed in his eyes, blinding him. He could barely make out the two shadowy figures that moved behind the light. There seemed to be two of them standing in the boat.

"Sophomore!" the strange voice said. "The time of initiation is at hand. Are you ready?"

Books in the *Horror High* series
Available from HarperPaperbacks

HORROR HIGH

Resolved: You're Dead

Nicholas Adams

HarperPaperbacks

A Division of HarperCollinsPublishers

HarperPaperbacks *A Division of* HarperCollins*Publishers*
10 East 53rd Street, New York, N.Y. 10022

Produced by Daniel Weiss Associates, Inc.
33 West 17th Street, New York, New York 10011.

First printing: December 1990

Manufactured in the United Kingdom by
HarperCollins*Publishers* Inc.

HarperPaperbacks and colophon are trademarks of
HarperCollins*Publishers*

10 9 8 7 6 5 4 3 2

Resolved:
You're Dead

Chapter 1

Lisa Enright lifted her eyes to the big clock that sat over the double doors of the Cresswell High auditorium. Her boyfriend Skip was going to be late. After fourth period, he had told Lisa that he needed to go to his car to pick up his notes before debating-team tryouts. Soon the bell would ring for fifth period, the time set aside every Friday for extracurricular activities. The end of September always brought the first meetings of the debating team. Skip was going to blow his chances by being late.

Lisa nervously brushed back her short-cropped black hair. She watched as the big hand on the clock drew closer to the top of the hour. Glancing back down the hall, she saw Mr. Ferris's corduroy blazer. John Ferris was the speech teacher and faculty adviser to the debating team. He was the final judge of who did or did not join the debating team.

Ferris brushed past Lisa and entered the auditorium. He had a reputation for being tough.

Lisa was almost sure that Ferris would disqualify anyone who arrived late to tryouts.

Lisa held her breath as she watched for Skip. Everyone knew there was only one real opening on the debating team. Skip, like Lisa, was a sophomore, a long shot to make the team. Jeffrey Goodman was the senior favorite to replace the one senior who had graduated the year before. Jeffrey had been the researcher for the team since his sophomore year.

"Hi, Lisa!"

She glanced up to see Bill Boland, another senior who had been on the team the year before. Bill smiled weakly at her. Tall, dark-haired with green eyes, Bill could be quiet and moody. Lisa knew he had a crush on her.

"Hi," Lisa replied. "Have you seen Skip?"

Bill frowned, shaking his head. "No. Lisa, I was wondering—er—well, the debating team always has a picnic after the first debate. We go out to Art's place, on the lake. Would you like to come along with me?"

Lisa smiled, but she wanted to make sure she didn't give him cause for optimism. "Thanks for the invitation, Bill, but Skip and I are going steady now."

"I don't see any ring," Bill said defensively.

"We don't need one," Lisa replied. "Our relationship is—"

"Hey, Billy boy, put it in gear!"

Art Lawing's voice echoed down the hall. He

came toward them with Donna Forsi walking beside him. Art and Donna had both been on the debating team the year before. As returning seniors, they were sure to be on the team again.

"We don't want to be late," Art said to Bill.

Art was a heavyset boy who carried himself with the confident arrogance of one who has gained early admission to college and dates a girl as pretty and smart as Donna.

"Who's your friend?" Art asked, winking at Lisa.

Lisa blushed and looked away, searching for Skip. She knew that Art had wooed Donna away from Bill two years ago, and she wasn't about to stroke his malicious ego.

"Are you trying out for the team?" Art asked Lisa.

Lisa shook her head. "No, I was . . ."

Donna smiled at her. "Forgive him. Mr. Ferris has been feeding him raw meat. I'm Donna Forsi."

Lisa smiled back. "Lisa Enright."

Donna smiled. She was athletic and bigboned, but her deep brown eyes, light-brown hair, and full lips made her one of the loveliest girls at Cresswell.

"Didn't you try out for cheerleader?" Donna asked.

Lisa shook her head. "No, that sort of thing doesn't really interest me."

"You're pretty enough to be a cheerleader," Bill offered.

"She's also too smart to fall for a line like that," Donna replied.

Bill blushed at the comment. "Sorry, I . . ."

"We're going to be late," Art said.

He pushed past Lisa, heading into the auditorium. Donna shook her head and followed him. Bill lingered for a moment, smiling at Lisa.

"Sure you don't want to try out for the team?" Bill asked.

Lisa shook her head. "Public speaking terrifies me."

"Oh. Well, see you later."

Bill went into the auditorium. Lisa looked back down the hall. Skip had two minutes before the bell.

Mr. Ferris was known for not playing favorites. Everyone, including the team members from the year before, had to prepare a one-minute speech about why they wanted to be on the team. Skip was going to miss out if he didn't hurry.

A few more hopeful orators went into the auditorium. The contestants were lining up on stage. Art was first in line. He was a lock to be the captain of the team. Lisa had felt uncomfortable with Art's manner, and she didn't understand why Donna would want to be with him.

"Let's quiet down," Mr. Ferris said as he eased into a chair.

Lisa sighed. The bell had not yet rung, but Skip was surely going to be late. As Lisa turned away from the door, she felt a hand falling on her shoulder.

"I made it!"

Lisa shook her head. "Skip Masters, you're cutting it close!"

Skip was breathing hard, as if he had been running. His sandy hair was ruffled, falling over his face. His blue eyes had grown wide with nervousness and anticipation. He clutched a jumbled mess of notebooks and textbooks against his chest. Lisa thought he was terribly cute.

"I had to go to my car," he said, holding up his three-by-five cards.

"I know," Lisa replied. "Hurry."

The notebooks fluttered to the floor. They both bent to pick them up. Suddenly, the bell rung shrilly overhead. Skip grimaced.

Lisa put her hand on his wrist. "Good luck."

Skip kissed her lightly on the cheek and then pushed into the auditorium. He ran down the aisle, bolting past Mr. Ferris, vaulting onto the stage. Lisa winced when she heard everyone laughing at Skip.

"Well," Mr. Ferris said dryly, "at least someone is showing some enthusiasm for our cause."

Everyone laughed, and Lisa felt embarrassed for Skip. But Skip didn't seem to mind. He was laughing and smiling at her from across the auditorium.

"All right," Mr. Ferris said. "Let's get started. Donna, why don't you lead off with your—"

Lisa had slipped into the rear of the auditorium. Mr. Ferris must have heard her. He stopped his instructions, standing up to look back at Lisa.

Lisa froze. She had only wanted to watch Skip give his speech.

"May I help you?" asked Mr. Ferris.

Suddenly, they were all staring at Lisa, waiting for her answer.

"Are you here to try out for the debating team?" Mr. Ferris asked impatiently. "Because you're late if you are."

Lisa shook her head. "No, I—"

"Well, then you'll have to leave," Mr. Ferris snapped. "This is a private team meeting."

As Lisa started to turn away, Donna spoke from the stage, helping her save face. "Mr. Ferris, didn't you say we need a recording secretary for the team's meetings?"

Mr. Ferris shrugged, shifting the wire-rimmed glasses that rode the bridge of his nose. "Well, yes," he replied. Then he turned back to Lisa. "You should have told me. Are you a friend of Donna's?"

"Yes, she is," Donna offered before Lisa could answer. "I thought I'd invite her to the meeting. Her name is Lisa Enright. I think she'd make a good secretary for the team."

"She has my vote," Bill chimed in.

"Me, too," Art said.

Mr. Ferris waved Lisa toward the front of the auditorium. "Come on, move into the first row. The recording secretary always takes down the minutes of the meeting. Right now, I need you to write down the names of all the people who audition."

Lisa hurried forward, opening one of Skip's notebooks. Skip was smiling at her from the stage. Art was also grinning, and Bill was staring at Lisa intently.

Lisa ignored Art and Bill and began to listen to Mr. Ferris explain the Forensic Award. This was a ten-thousand-dollar scholarship, awarded each year to one of the seniors on the debating team. The endowment had come from a wealthy graduate of Cresswell High School. Mr. Ferris, along with two English teachers, would select the winner.

Finally, Mr. Ferris sat down and Donna began her speech. Lisa sat through one speech after another, waiting for Skip's turn.

"Time!" Mr. Ferris called impatiently, cutting off a terrible speech, and startling Lisa. "Okay, Jeffrey. You're up."

Jeffrey Goodman cleared his throat and began his speech in a high voice. The words came out clearly, crisply. His oration was not stirring, but it came across as sincere. He kept the speech under a minute, making his point in fifty-eight seconds.

Mr. Ferris nodded appreciatively. "Well done, Jeffrey. You've come a long way. A long way."

Jeffrey smirked as he left the stage. He joined the others at the rear of the auditorium. Art and Bill offered their congratulations.

Mr. Ferris stood up. "Well, I suppose that's it."

Donna pointed toward Skip. "There's one more, Mr. Ferris."

He peered back toward the stage, frowning. "Oh. The tardy one."

Lisa sunk lower in her chair when she heard the tone of Mr. Ferris's voice. Skip had come out of the shadows. He stood quietly at the lectern.

"Let's get it over with," Mr. Ferris said impatiently.

Chapter 2

"And in conclusion," Skip Masters said confidently, "without the interchange of new ideas, without the heated voices of debate to examine *both* sides of an issue, the human race could be doomed to a loss of spirit, and the very fabric of freedom itself would be threatened! Thank you."

Skip stepped away from the podium. He flinched when he heard applause. At first he thought Lisa was clapping. But then he saw that Mr. Ferris had risen from his seat to put his hands together.

"Bravo. What was your name again?"

"Skip Masters."

"Excellent," Mr. Ferris said. "A fine job."

Skip stole a quick glance at Lisa. She nodded, giving him the victory sign. Skip had stunned everyone. His audition speech had clearly been the best of the new students' speeches.

The team veterans were impressed. Art was frowning, though. He always hated to be outdone by anyone, much less a new kid who was wet behind the ears.

Skip knew he had aced the tryout. Mr. Ferris had let the speech go on for nearly two minutes. Lisa's looks of adoration were the frosting on the cake.

Jeffrey glared at Skip and started out of the auditorium.

"Hold on, Jeffrey," Mr. Ferris said. "I need all the team members here. Come on down, all of you."

Jeffrey hesitated, looking hopeful. "You mean—"

"In the front row," Mr. Ferris told them. "Hurry. We're almost out of time."

Art, Bill, Donna, and Jeffrey, along with the other aspirants, moved down to join Skip and Lisa in the first row of seats. Bill hung his head. Art put his arm around Donna, who immediately removed it from her shoulder. Jeffrey cast sideways looks at Skip and Mr. Ferris. Skip and Lisa avoided looking at each other, because they didn't want Mr. Ferris to know they were going steady, at least not right away.

The faculty adviser smiled. "Art, you're captain this year. Bill, you've made the team again. Donna, you'll be our lead speaker in the first debate. Skip, you're last but not least. We're going to need your energy."

Mr. Ferris smiled at Jeffrey, who was slouching in a chair. "You're the first alternate, Jeffrey. And we'll need you on research again. We're counting on you."

Jeffrey nodded blankly. "Sure."

Mr. Ferris looked at Art. "Art, I heard that you were going to be appointed treasurer of the student council, to replace the boy who moved away last week."

"No way," Art replied. "I'm sticking with the debating team exclusively. Nothing is going to interfere with that."

"Good," Mr. Ferris replied. "Lisa, did you record the team as stated?"

Lisa stood up to read her notes. "Art Lawing, captain. Bill Boland. Donna Forsi, lead speaker, first debate. Skip Masters. Jeffrey Goodman, first alternate and researcher."

Mr. Ferris nodded approvingly. "That's it. From now on, we meet every morning before school, except Fridays, when we meet fifth period."

Lisa kept writing it all down. Everything had worked out for the best. Skip had done well under pressure, and somehow she had ended up as the secretary of the team.

Art raised his hand. "What's our topic for the first debate?"

Mr. Ferris looked from one to another. "Resolved: The Soviet Union should retain control of its dissident republics and satellite states by any means possible."

Art rubbed his hands together. "Great. I can

get into a little Commie bashing. Russia look out."

Mr. Ferris shook his head. "Hold on. We might have to argue on behalf of the Soviet Union's keeping control of the satellite states. And we only have ten days to prepare."

Donna leaned back, looking worried. "Then we better get started. Ten days isn't a very long time."

When the meeting adjourned, Lisa sought out Donna to thank her for getting her onto the team. As they were talking, Art moved in to whisk Donna away. Bill followed them like a faithful puppy.

After Mr. Ferris left, Skip and Lisa were alone with Jeffrey. Lisa could tell that Jeffrey was upset at being relegated to the position of researcher once again.

Skip extended his hand to Jeffrey. "Congratulations on first alternate, Jeff."

"Jeffrey. I like to be called Jeffrey."

"Okay, Jeffrey. No hard feelings?"

Jeffrey hesitated. Lisa felt better when he finally shook hands with Skip. After they had shaken, Jeffrey left in a hurry. His uneasiness could not stop Skip and Lisa from being ecstatic.

She smiled at him. "Congratulations."

Skip took her hand. "I couldn't have done it without you."

"No," Lisa teased. "You couldn't."

Skip grinned. "Pretty wild, huh, the way Donna got you into the club."

"She's sweet," Lisa replied. "And pretty."

"Not as pretty as you," Skip said.

Their eyes locked. Skip lowered his mouth, kissing her lightly. They embraced triumphantly.

"I'm proud of you," Lisa said. "You beat out Jeffrey, and he's a senior."

"Hey," Skip replied, drawing back. "Why don't we meet in the library after school. We can get a jump on the topic."

"It's a date," she replied with a smile.

They started to kiss again, but the bell rang for sixth period. They hurried out of the auditorium.

Chapter 3

The final meeting before the first debate was held on Sunday at Art Lawing's house. The debate fell on the following day, the last Monday of September. The mood of the team had been subdued during the regular Friday meeting. Mock debates were one thing; facing a real opponent was another. Central High, their first opponent, had a reputation for producing good debaters.

The Lawings lived on Storm Lake, a long, wide body of inland water about twenty miles outside Cresswell. Lisa and Skip drove to the meeting in Skip's mother's car. He had just turned sixteen and was proud to be driving.

As the station wagon maneuvered along the winding, lakeside road, Lisa gazed out the window at the first signs of color in the fall foliage. The red, yellow, and orange tones were beginning to show in the shadowy afternoon light. They ascended a rise that gave them a breathtaking view of Storm Lake.

Skip let out a sigh.

"What's wrong?" Lisa asked.

Skip shrugged. "I don't know. I just don't see why we had to have the picnic thing today."

"It's not a picnic," Lisa replied. "It's a work meeting. Mr. Ferris wants to make sure we're ready for tomorrow. Are you nervous?"

Skip nodded. "Big time. Our first debate."

As they turned a steep corner, Lisa saw something that might take Skip's mind off his stage fright. "Look," she said, pointing out over the lake. "Pine Island."

Skip glanced quickly to his left. He could see a small land mass on the other side of the lake. For a moment, both of them could see the silhouette of a house in the middle of the island.

"The old Bigelow estate," Lisa said. "I forgot all about it. I haven't been up here in a couple of years."

Skip shook off the chill that ran through his shoulders. "They say no one ever found Mrs. Bigelow's head."

Lisa laughed a little. "That was before we were born. I think they told us that story at summer camp just to scare us. I don't even think it's true."

"No one has lived there since it happened," Skip offered. "They say they never found the ax he used to kill her."

Lisa patted his arm. "Don't worry. I'm here to protect you."

"Thanks a lot!"

"I think that's the road," Lisa said.

Skip turned onto a private drive marked LAWING. They drove slowly through a stretch of wooded land, emerging onto a huge circular driveway that was filled with cars. The Lawing house was a massive, beam-and-glass modern structure. Lisa had seen such homes only in magazines.

They climbed out of the car. Art came out to meet them. He announced that Mr. Ferris and the others had already arrived. And Mr. Ferris was ready to work.

After two hours of discussion and rehearsal of speeches defending opposing sides of the issue, Mr. Ferris closed his notebook and stood up.

"I think that's it. Any questions?" he said.

The debating team seemed ready. They had gone over their material three times. The afternoon shadows were growing long outside Art Lawing's spacious living room.

"This meeting is adjourned," Mr. Ferris said. "Let's get Central."

As they stood up, Art's mother came in. She was a gracious, well-mannered woman who invited them all to dinner. Mr. Ferris declined, but Art talked the rest of the team into staying.

"I need someone to stir the soup," Mrs. Lawing announced sweetly. "Art's father is watching the news. I can't tear him away from the television in his study."

"I can help," Skip said quickly.

He wanted to make a good impression, since he was the newest member of the team. Donna also followed Mrs. Lawing into the kitchen to help. Bill and Jeffrey immediately broke out a chessboard and began to set up the pieces. Lisa offered to play the winner, since she was also interested in chess.

When she felt a cold hand on her wrist, she turned to see Art beside her. Art began to pull her toward the front door.

"Come on, I want to show you something," he said.

Lisa wanted to protest, but she didn't feel like making a scene. It was innocent enough, even though Art was creepy and overbearing.

Art led her out the front door. They walked in silence across the grass that stretched to the shore of Storm Lake. At the edge of the water, Art stopped and pointed toward Pine Island. "You know what's over there?"

Lisa sighed. "Yes, the Bigelow estate. I know all about it. They never found her head. We've all heard the story."

Art turned to smile at her. "The team is looking good," he said softly.

"Yes," she replied. *What a weirdo,* she thought.

He squinted at her. "Well? Am I the best or what?"

"I don't know," Lisa replied indifferently. "At this point, I think it's ridiculous to make such comparisons, unless you just want to boost your ego."

Art gestured toward a boat that was moored at his family's dock. "We could ride over to Pine Island," he said. "There's still enough light. We could look for Mrs. Bigelow's head."

Lisa glared at him. "Art, what's going on here?"

Art shrugged. "I thought we should get to know one another."

"Donna is my friend," Lisa shot back. "I hope you're not—"

Art grabbed her arms. He pulled her toward him, trying to kiss her. Lisa pushed him away. Art stepped back and lost his balance. He reached out, but there was nothing to grab hold of. He went down on his backside in a foot of water.

"You did that on purpose!" he cried as he scrambled to his feet.

"Serves you right!" Lisa said. "I'm going to tell Donna about this, Art. She's my friend."

"No!" he replied. "It'll ruin the debate."

But Lisa was already walking back toward the house, leaving Art to pull himself together. When she came into Mrs. Lawing's kitchen, she saw Skip stirring the pot. He smiled at her.

Lisa turned toward Donna, who was busy making a salad. Suddenly she couldn't think of the words to tell Donna that Art had tried to kiss her. If she blurted out the truth, it would upset the happy atmosphere of the party. The truth would only bring everyone down.

"Where's Art?" Mrs. Lawing asked.

Lisa hesitated. "I don't know. I think he took a walk by the lake."

"I hope he was wearing his sweater," Mrs. Lawing said.

Lisa nodded and looked at Donna again. Donna smiled as she tossed the salad with large wooden spoons. For all his arrogance, Art had been right. A confession by Lisa would only upset the team before their first big debate. Lisa would have to wait awhile before she told Donna that her boyfriend had made a pass at her by the lake.

Chapter 4

Lisa sat next to Jeffrey, peering toward the Central High School stage. The debate was almost underway. Cresswell's team sat under the lights. They had come all the way across town to do verbal battle with the team on the other side of the proscenium. Central High was going to be the home team for the first contest.

"They look nervous," Lisa whispered to Jeffrey. "Especially Skip. He's as white as a ghost."

Jeffrey looked up from his writing pad. He had given all his notes to the team. Now it was up to them to deliver the arguments.

"I hope Skip does all right," Lisa said.

Jeffrey shrugged. "It's his first debate. He'll be fine, though," he said casually.

The moderator stepped up to the microphone. After introductions, he stated the topic: The Soviet Union should retain control of its republics. Central would argue against the proposition. Cresswell had to take the affirmative, pro-Soviet side. Central would go first in the debate.

Jeffrey leaned back in his chair. "They're on their own."

Lisa sensed a smug tone in his voice. She poked him in the arm as a reprimand.

"Stop it," he said. "The debate is about to begin."

Lisa peered toward the stage. Skip looked seasick. Lisa hoped he could get through the debate without causing disaster for Cresswell. She would settle for that, even if Cresswell didn't win.

"Furthermore," said the captain of the Central High team, "to deny the Soviet republics their sovereignty would be like the federal government denying the states of the union their basic right to freedom and regional identity. The right of self-determination is the right of each state to form its own government, to seek freedom for its own people. Let them go, Mr. Gorbachev. Free the people while you still have the chance!"

A slight titter spread through the crowd. The judges, all from the local media, were nodding and making notes. The debate had been seesawing back and forth. Nobody seemed to be winning or losing.

Lisa looked at Jeffrey. "Is it bad?"

Jeffrey sighed. "Central came prepared."

Lisa looked at Mr. Ferris. He looked worried.

Art and Donna had been good, but Central was holding its own.

"We can't be far behind," Lisa said.

Jeffrey exhaled. "We should have saved Art for last instead of Skip."

Lisa glanced at Art. He sat back in his chair, smiling with confidence. Lisa hadn't told anyone about his pass at her. She had begun to think that it might be better if she just forgot the whole thing.

Jeffrey nodded toward the stage. "Let's see how Bill does with the notes I gave him."

Bill Boland stepped slowly behind the podium. His hands fumbled for a moment with the three-by-five cards. Jeffrey cringed when Bill dropped the cards and they fluttered to the stage.

Bill hurried to pick them up, but the damage was already done. He gave his speech blankly, without passion. By the time he sat down, the judges were squirming impatiently in their seats.

Lisa looked at Mr. Ferris. His expression was dour. He sunk lower in his seat as the Central High debater launched another forceful attack against the leader of the Soviet Union. The judges were suddenly enthralled by the speaker at the podium.

When the speaker sat down again, Lisa looked nervously toward the stage. "This is it," she said under her breath. "It's all up to Skip."

Skip seemed calm and collected as he stepped up to the podium. He looked at his three-by-five cards for a moment. Suddenly he put the cards back into the pocket of his suitcoat.

"What's he doing?" Jeffrey said. "He can't wing it."

Skip put his hands on the podium and then stared out at the judges. "The issue," he said clearly, "is not the control of the satellite states by a central power, but rather the strengthening of a nation's unity."

One of the judges leaned forward, suddenly interested. Mr. Ferris sat up straight. Lisa was full of hope.

Skip's voice swelled in the auditorium. "My distinguished competitor invoked the name of Mr. Gorbachev, a great leader by any standard. But I feel inclined to invoke another name, a leader by the name of Abraham Lincoln."

Jeffrey frowned. "What's he doing?"

"Shhh!" Lisa didn't want to miss a word.

"And like Mr. Lincoln, Mr. Gorbachev is fighting to hold his country together. He recognizes that there is strength in unity. That emancipation, true freedom, is earned by staying together. The whole is greater than the sum of its parts. . . . The Soviet Union is fighting, not for the continued subjugation of its ethnic minorities, but rather for the strengthening of the union. . . . Only when the nation is strong can the individual republics stand on their own."

All of the judges had begun to pay attention. Central's captain had a worried look on her face. Lisa could feel the crowd shifting toward Skip's point of view. He had them! Even Mr. Ferris had cracked a smile.

"Strength in unity," Skip went on. "Lincoln recognized the need. That was how he held the country together. Like our own states, the Soviet states revolve around a rigid hub. Rather than cutting them loose, Mr. Gorbachev must pull them in, like prodigals who must return home. Then, when they are strong on their own, they can let true freedom take root. Personal liberty and national pride can flourish. The union can survive, and the spokes will guarantee the continued turning of the wheel's hub. Thank you."

A hush fell over the auditorium. Lisa took the silence to be a bad sign. The judges were putting their heads together. Had Cresswell blown the first debate of the year?

"What do you think?" Lisa whispered to Jeffrey.

"It's okay," Jeffrey replied. "Your boy did fine. He didn't use my notes, but he does have a passionate delivery."

Lisa saw the moderator stepping up to the podium. "They've made their decision."

"May I have your attention," the moderator

said. "The judges vote three to two in favor of Cresswell. Resolved: The Soviet Union *should* maintain control over its republics."

The audience burst into applause. On stage, the Cresswell debate team went wild. Art hugged Donna. Bill shook hands with Skip, telling him he had saved the day. They had won the debate on Skip's final argument.

Lisa and Jeffrey found their way onto the stage. Jeffrey began to lecture Bill about his mistakes. Mr. Ferris moved around, patting everyone on the back.

When Skip saw Lisa, he held out his arms. She ran to him, embracing. She was so proud of him. Their lips touched for a few seconds.

Skip was the hero of the day. No one suspected that the sandy-haired boy would soon be in deep trouble.

Chapter 5

On Saturday morning, Skip Masters lay in his room, exhausted from the tough week after the first debate. Despite the victory, the debating team had continued to meet every morning before school, including an early session on Friday before they held their regular fifth-period meeting.

Mr. Ferris was a driving force, something Skip respected. He made the team argue both sides of several subjects. They were not sure of the topic for the next debate, which was still three weeks away. Mr. Ferris pushed Bill the hardest, since he was the one who obviously needed the most work.

Skip replayed the week in his mind. No one at Cresswell had treated him like a conquering hero. Debating wasn't exactly the favorite sport of the Cresswell student body. Art had received most of the recognition, since he was a senior and the captain of the team.

But Skip still felt pride in a job well done. He had saved the debate, but he had not let it go to his head. He knew there was more hard work ahead, evenings in the library with Lisa in addition to his regular homework. Lisa was becoming something of a researcher herself. She was really helping the team.

"Skip!" His mother was calling from downstairs. "Skip, you better hurry before all the pancakes are gone."

Skip didn't reply. He just lay there, staring up at the ceiling. Upon waking, Skip had found himself filled with an inexplicable sense of dread. He had tried to go back to sleep, but he knew there was something he had to do. What was it that he—

"The picnic," he said aloud.

The debating team was having its annual picnic at Art's place. Skip took a deep breath. He had spent the whole week with the debating team. Maybe he needed a break from his colleagues.

Skip thought about each member of the team. He liked Donna the best. She had become good friends with Lisa. She had a sweet nature, and she was smart and steadfast. Skip couldn't figure out what Donna saw in Art.

Art bothered Skip. Art always had to be in charge. Like a bull gorilla, Art had to have the last word. Skip did not like being in such juvenile competition with one of the members of his own team. But sometimes he could feel Art's jealousy toward anyone who might outshine him. Just the same, he couldn't think of anything in particular that Art had done to offend him.

Bill and Jeffrey were still fairly cold to Skip. He understood their feelings. Skip had taken Jeffrey's place on the team, and Bill's hopes of dating Lisa had been dashed. It really didn't bother him that they were aloof.

Skip felt some tension at the meetings, but he chalked it up to the pride of not wanting to lose. Everyone seemed to accept him as part of the winning process. But except for Donna, Skip couldn't say that he called the other team members true friends. And he wasn't sure that he wanted to spend his free Saturday with these people.

"Skip!"

"I don't want any breakfast, Mom!"

"No, honey, it's Lisa. She's on the phone."

Skip rolled out of bed. He had not heard the telephone ring. When he got to the hall phone, he picked up the extension and muttered hello.

Lisa hesitated at the other end of the line. "Skip? Is that you?"

"Yeah. What's up, Leez?"

"You don't sound like yourself."

"I'm beat," Skip replied. "This week did me in."

"We've got the picnic this afternoon," Lisa offered.

Skip sighed. "Leez, I'm not sure I want to go to that picnic."

"Really?" She sounded disappointed. "Why?"

"I don't know. Let's hit a movie and then go for burgers."

"Skip, they're expecting you. You're the new star of the team."

"They saw me all week," he said defensively. "Maybe I want to spend some time alone with you."

"Aw, that's sweet. But you have to go. If you don't, they'll all think you don't like them."

"Except for Donna, I'm not sure I do like any of them. And they don't seem to like me."

"That's not true, Skip."

"Then why are they so cold?" he asked.

"We've been working hard," she replied. "Now we can loosen up a little. You'll see. It'll be fun."

"I don't know, Leez," he said. "Let's do something else, just the two of us. Hey, I know. There's a Bogart festival at Porterville. And it's still warm enough to walk on the beach."

Lisa sighed. "I want to go to the picnic, Skip. I'm supposed to help Mrs. Lawing with the food."

"That's another thing. Why do we always have to party at Art's? I mean, just because he's got a nice house on a lake—"

"Please, Skip. Don't."

They were on the verge of a fight. Skip could feel it. He didn't want to mess up his relationship with Lisa over some stupid picnic.

"Okay," he said defeatedly. "What time should I pick you up?"

"How about eleven? The picnic starts at noon."

He looked at the clock in his parents' room. "It's nine-thirty now. I guess I can watch Pee Wee and still make it by eleven."

"Great," Lisa said in a happy tone.

"See you then."

"Skip?"

"Yeah?"

"I love you."

"And I you. See you at eleven."

He hung up the phone.

"If you really loved me," he said to himself, "you wouldn't make me go to this stupid party."

Chapter 6

Lisa sat in the front seat of the station wagon, staring dreamily at the glowing landscape as it passed by. The deep-purple waters of the lake reflected the fall colors of the higher ground. It was going to be a perfect Indian-summer day for the debating-team picnic.

"What a difference a couple of weeks can make," she said to Skip. "It's so beautiful out here."

Skip had not shaken his ill humor. "If you say so."

Lisa made a face, frowning playfully. "Aw, is him going to be a big baby grumpus all day?"

"It's not too late to go to Porterville," Skip offered gruffly.

Lisa patted his hand. "Relax. Enjoy the scenery. We're not going to work today. We're going to have fun."

Skip suddenly let out a ripping scream.

"Why did you do that?" Lisa asked.

"You said *fun*. It's Pee Wee's secret word today. And when anyone says the secret word, you're supposed to—"

"Scream real loud!" Lisa replied. "Real mature, Masters."

They both laughed. Lisa slid closer to him on the car seat. Skip put his arm around her. She would never let him stay in a bad mood for long.

Skip's eyes grew wider when the car rounded a long curve. "Wow, even Pine Island looks beautiful today. The old house is shining."

Lisa turned to look out over the lake, but Pine Island was no longer visible from the car window. She thought about the pass Art had made at her. She was anxious to see if he would keep his promise not to get fresh with her. If he tried it again, Lisa planned to tell everyone.

"Hey," Skip said. "You know what I like most about this picnic?"

"What?"

"You're going to be there."

"There's the turnoff," she said.

The station wagon rolled slowly up the driveway, which was already full of cars. Apparently, the picnic was underway.

"He must have invited other people," Lisa said. "Look at all the cars."

"Porterville?" Skip asked.

Lisa opened her car door. "We're already here. Let's give it a try."

Skip shook his head. "I guess this is why they call it going steady."

"What?"

"I said I'm ready."

He got out of the car. They held hands until they got inside. The Lawing grounds were covered with juniors and seniors from Cresswell. Lisa and Skip would be the only sophomores.

Art watched as Skip and Lisa walked toward the water. "Look at him," he said to Bill and Jeffrey, who were standing with him on the lawn. "He thinks he's so hot."

Bill sighed, shaking his head. "He's a wimp. He doesn't deserve a girl like Lisa."

"He's not so bad," Jeffrey offered. "He's a good debater."

Art grimaced. "Yeah, you're right. But he didn't even come over to say hello to us."

"He took your spot on the team," Bill said to Jeffrey. "How can you defend him like that?"

"What's he done to you?" Jeffrey challenged. "He can't help it if Lisa prefers him to you, Boland. It's his luck. And he beat me fair and square. Let's face it, he's a better speaker."

"You haven't gone out of your way to be nice to him," Bill replied to Jeffrey. "Are you telling me you're starting to like him?"

"The name of the game is winning, Boland. Skip saved our butts at Central."

Bill bristled and scowled at Jeffrey. "Are you saying I blew that debate?"

"No," Art broke in. "He's saying you almost blew it."

Bill hung his head. "You're right. Okay, I admit it. But it won't happen again. I promise you that."

"Cheer up," Jeffrey replied. "It was an honest mistake."

Art was still staring at Skip and Lisa. Bill saw the sly smile on Art's face.

"What are you thinking?" he asked.

"Well, we don't want to hurt old Skippy there, but we can have a little fun with him."

"Count me out," Jeffrey said, walking away.

Bill seemed intrigued. "Let's hear it."

Art watched the clouds building to the north. "Later."

They began to mix with the growing crowd of students. Art kept his eye on Skip, waiting for the right time. When the storm blew the party inside, Art finally got his chance.

Dark, thunderous clouds swept down from the north, emptying heavy sheets of rain over Pine Island and the rest of Storm Lake. Picnickers scattered toward shelter. Some of them grabbed food to take with them into Art's huge living room. Thirty or so wet teenagers crowded together, many of them holding potato salad, cartons of soda, potato chips, and packages of uncooked hot dogs.

Lisa trudged through the throng carrying a bowl of strawberry gelatin. Her hair was plastered to her head. She found Skip standing next to Donna. They were both holding bags of hot-dog buns. They laughed when they saw Lisa with the bowl of gelatin.

Lisa laughed with them. "This is crazy!"

Donna made a sweeping gesture with the bag of buns. "These are some of Art's friends from the country club. I can't stand most of them, but Art thought it might liven things up to invite them."

Skip looked hopeful. "Now we have a good excuse to blow out of here. If we hurry, we can catch the evening show of *Casablanca* in Porterville."

Lisa nodded. "Okay, but let's wait a little while. We can't hurry in this storm. And I need to dry my hair before we go anywhere." She turned to Donna. "Care to join us?"

"Sure," Donna replied.

Skip frowned. "Will Art be coming with us?"

"No," Donna replied. "He'll want to party with his friends. It's okay, we have an understanding. Besides, these lounge lizards aren't going anywhere as long as there's free food."

Donna turned away to look for Mrs. Lawing.

Lisa looked up at Skip with her brown eyes.

"Maybe I should have listened to you about Porterville."

Skip blushed and smiled. "No, I've been the jerk. A real dweeb-o-matic. Any chance of you forgiving me?"

"Oh, I'd say about a hundred percent chance."

They kissed over the bowl of strawberry gelatin.

Skip looked toward the back of the house. "Let me see if I can find you something to dry off with."

Lisa watched him disappear into a dark hallway. Skip was so sweet. They would leave as soon as the storm let up. Until then, they were prisoners of the rain and the thunder.

Chapter 7

Skip stepped cautiously through the shadows of the hallway. He had been lost for a few minutes in the maze of the house. He thought for a moment that he had seen Donna, but then she was gone. He could hear the rain above him, pounding on the roof. His feet shuffled along the thick carpet.

"Hello," he called into a dimly lit room, from which he could hear soft voices.

The lights flickered and then died. The lone hallway light behind him was suddenly doused. He was standing in a pitch-black room. He reached out to touch the walls. He thought he could hear someone breathing in the recesses of the room. But the voices had gone mute.

"Anybody there?"

Something bumped around the dark corner.

"Hello," Skip said in a louder voice.

Nothing.

"All right, this isn't funny."

He turned back toward the hallway. Then he heard a rustling voice, and someone slipped a cloth bag over Skip's head. Two pairs of hands grabbed his arms. They began to drag him down the hall.

"What is this?" Skip cried.

A gag was pressed forcefully against his mouth. Skip tried to shout, but it was no use. He had to go along with his captors.

They dragged him through the shadows of the house, down a flight of stairs, and out a door. Then he felt the cool air and rain as he was taken outside. They moved across the lawn, toward the lake. Skip figured they were taking him to the boathouse. It was some kind of prank. It had to be.

He felt the dock beneath his feet. A door opened. They pushed him into the boathouse. Skip was pushed down onto some kind of wooden crate.

"What is this?" he gasped through the gag.

"Silence," a strange voice replied. "The time has come for the initiation!"

Thunder rolled over Storm Lake. The wind tossed breaking whitecaps on the surface of the turbulent water. Paper plates and napkins from the picnic rode the stiff gale, whirling in the air until they landed on a tree or a shrub. The storm was so bad that no one had left the party yet.

Lisa stood at the front window, peering into the wall of rain. She thought for a moment that she saw several shapes moving across the lawn toward the lake. But just then, Donna tapped her on the shoulder, offering her a dry towel. When Lisa turned back to the window, the shapes were gone.

"What are you looking at?" Donna asked.

Lisa began to dry her hair. "Nothing. This storm is playing tricks on me. It's spooky."

Donna sighed. "Yes, I guess it's making everyone a little weird."

"What's wrong?"

"It's Art." Donna replied with a serious expression on her pretty face. "He and Bill were hanging out upstairs. Art got really flippant with me when I told him he should come downstairs and take care of his guests."

"Maybe he just needs to be apart from things for a while," said Lisa, trying to put the best light on the situation. Remembering her own experience with Art, she knew that any grievance Donna had with him must be justified.

Donna looked at her. "Lisa, may I talk to you about something? I mean, I feel as if we're really becoming friends."

"I do, too," Lisa said softly.

"I trust you, and I have to talk to someone," Donna went on. "I need another perspective on things."

Lisa stopped drying her hair. "I'm listening, Donna."

"It's Art. I don't know what to do. I think I

want to stop dating him. It's just not working out."

Lisa hesitated, wondering if Donna had somehow found out about the pass Art had made. "Donna, you should think this over."

"I have," Donna replied. "I just don't care about Art like—well, like the way you care about Skip. I mean, you guys can at least talk to each other."

"Can't you talk to Art?"

"Not anymore. I feel bad, Lisa. Two years ago, when we first joined the debating team, Art went after me. I had dated Bill a few times, but that didn't amount to anything. Art was so handsome and smart. It seemed natural for a while, but now I'm not so sure about us as a couple."

"Is there someone else?" Lisa asked.

"No, not really. I just don't want to be with Art anymore. I—"

Loud voices rose on the other side of the room, reminding Donna that they were in a room full of Art's friends. "Maybe this isn't the time or place," she said.

Lisa nodded. "You can ride home with us. Hey, where is Skip, anyway?"

"There's Mrs. Lawing. Maybe she knows."

They approached Art's mother to ask if she had seen Skip. Mrs. Lawing replied that Art and some of the other boys had gone down to the boathouse to make sure the boat was secure in the storm. Lisa figured that Art and Skip had been the shapes in the rain.

"Maybe we should go check on them," Lisa offered.

"They'll be fine," Mrs. Lawing replied. "Let them have their fun. The boathouse is closed in. They'll be out of the rain."

"Sure," Donna rejoined with a grimace, "boy stuff."

Lisa smiled nervously. "You're right. What could possibly happen?" She knew that the minute Skip came back they would leave. She didn't want to stay around any longer.

Chapter 8

They tied Skip's hands and feet to the crate. The cloth bag was ripped from his head. Suddenly a bright light flashed in his eyes, blinding him. He could barely make out the two shadowy figures that moved behind the light. There seemed to be two of them standing in Art's boat.

"Sophomore!" the strange voice said. "The time of initiation is at hand. Are you ready?"

The voice seemed to be electronically altered, as if it was coming out of some kind of speaker. Skip knew that Art had a portable microphone that would play through any FM radio. They had used the device in their mock debates.

The eerie voice rose in the boathouse, but it no longer frightened Skip. "Your moment of judgment is at hand, sophomore. The senior council decrees that you must perform a task of our bidding."

The gag was pulled away from Skip's mouth. Even if he shouted, nobody would hear. The sound of the waves and thunder would muffle his cries for help. But what a chicken he would be if he cried for help. He could deal with this on his own.

"This is like a class thing, right?" he said sarcastically. "I'm the new sophomore, so the seniors gang up on me. Is that it, Art?"

"Silence! A newcomer must brave the challenge. He must prove himself worthy by facing an initiation of fire."

Skip squinted into the light. Art's father was the lake warden, which was probably why the boat had been equipped with a searchlight. It was really a stupid gag. Art was capable of better.

"You have to face your trial," the voice said. "You must finish your act of labor."

"Who do you think I am?" Skip asked. "Hercules?"

"Silence!"

Skip was having trouble taking the whole thing seriously. At least until his hands began to hurt. They had tied him too tightly.

He squirmed on the crate. "This is really unnecessary, guys. If you want to haze me a little, I can take it. But forget the rough stuff."

"Silence! As a sophomore, you must perform the sacred rite of initiation. It has been decreed."

A silence fell over the boathouse. Skip had

begun to sweat. The little joke wasn't getting any funnier.

"Let me loose," he told them. "I'm cool on this, guys. I won't tell anyone about it. Just don't get creepy on me."

The silence prevailed.

Someone stepped up onto the dock, next to Skip. He was wearing a black hood over his head. His body was covered by a black robe.

"Are you the grand inquisitor?" Skip asked flippantly.

"Silence, sophomore!"

Skip's eyes grew wide as a thin, silver blade flashed in the beam of the spotlight. "No!" he cried.

The hooded figure raised the knife.

Skip screamed, but no one could hear him over the roar of the storm.

Then the edge of the blade slid over the ropes. Suddenly Skip's hands and feet were free. As he rubbed his wrists, the hooded figure jumped back into the boat.

"Do you accept the challenge, or do you want everyone to know you're a wimp?" the electric voice asked. "Do you have the courage to face the initiation?"

Skip grimaced, shaking his head. It had to be Art and Bill, or maybe Jeffrey, behind the light. They were trying to have some fun with him.

But Skip wondered if he might be able to

turn the tables on them and come out the winner.

"Sophomore!" the voice said again. "Are you prepared to meet the challenge of the initiation?"

Skip started to reply, but a bucket of cold lake water splashed over him. He fought to maintain his composure as he wiped his face. Skip was not going to let Art win. If Art wanted real competition, he would get it back double. Skip would see the prank through to the end!

"Are you ready, sophomore? You must prove yourself in the face of danger."

Skip didn't like the sound of the word *danger*. But surely Art and the others would not put him in a situation where he might get hurt. They were just trying to mess with his head.

"Are you prepared?"

"What do I have to do?" Skip asked.

Something flew through the air. A woolen scarf landed on Skip's lap. It bore the school colors of Cresswell High. The scarves were sold in the bookstore in town.

"Your task, sophomore, is to take that scarf to Pine Island tonight!"

Skip frowned. "Pine Island?"

"Go to the old Bigelow estate—"

"Why, do you want me to look for Mrs. Bigelow's head?" Skip asked.

Another bucket of cold water splashed over

him. Skip wiped his face. He was losing patience. He wanted the hazing to be finished.

"Take the scarf," the electric voice told him. "Go inside the old Bigelow house. Tie the scarf to one of the basement rafters. That will prove your courage and your loyalty to Cresswell."

Skip lifted the scarf. "How will you know I put it there?"

"Tomorrow morning, the basement will be checked. Only then will you be considered one of the brotherhood."

After Skip was gone, Bill laughed, slapping his hand on his knee. "Did you see his face? His eyes were bugging out."

Art sighed, shaking his head. "He was scared at first, but then he caught on to us."

They were still sitting in the boathouse, trying to enjoy the game they had played on Skip. Art had come up with the plan on the spur of the moment. He wished he had been able to arrange something a little more frightening.

Bill seemed more happy with their efforts to get Skip riled. "We smoked him, Lawing. He'll never take that scarf over to the Bigelow house. He'll chicken out before he ever finds a boat."

Art leaned back with his hands behind his head. "Maybe not. He was smiling at the end. I think he might try it."

A sudden look of anguish spread over Bill's weak face. "Hey, wait a minute. What if he asks somebody about this bogus initiation you dreamed up? He might go to Mr. Ferris and rat on us."

Art shook his head. "He won't."

"How can you be so sure?"

"Didn't you see his face?" Art replied. "He was cocky. He thinks he's going to show us up. It makes me glad we tried to haze him. One good debate and he thinks he's a star. He might try to go to Pine Island."

"Nah," Bill replied, "he'll never do it. At night? With the lake so rough? He's a wuss. When we check in the morning, that scarf won't be anywhere near the Bigelow house."

"We'll see," Art replied.

Chapter 9

Lisa was shaking her head. "I still say that Ingrid Bergman should have stayed with Humphrey Bogart at the end. That French guy was a wimp."

Skip stared straight ahead at the dark interstate highway. "No way. The war is underway. Bogie has to do the noble thing, and that means giving her up. She has to leave with the French guy."

They had been arguing about *Casablanca* all the way from Porterville. The rain had stopped, making the way home easier. It was almost eleven o'clock as they approached the Cresswell exit. Skip guided the car down the ramp and turned onto a side street.

"She loved Bogie," Lisa went on. "She should have stayed with him."

"They have to sacrifice their love because of the war," Skip insisted. "Isn't that right, Donna?"

Donna had been sitting quietly in the back

seat. She didn't seem to hear him. She was gazing out the window.

"Donna?"

"This is my street," Donna said. "Turn there."

They dropped her in front of an old Victorian house on Washington Street. She thanked them absently and then ran into the house. Lisa sighed as Skip pulled the station wagon away from the curb.

"What's wrong with her?" Skip asked. "She didn't say two words on the ride back. Is she okay?"

"It's Art. They're having troubles. Donna wants to stop dating him, but she doesn't know how to tell him. She's afraid it could mess up the team."

Skip exhaled, nodding his head. "She's right about that. It may have an effect on the next debate."

"Skip? What do you think about Art?"

"Well, I think Donna's too good for him," he said. "Sometimes he can be an arrogant jerk."

"He's kind of creepy sometimes," Lisa said. She broke down and started to cry.

"Lisa, what's wrong?"

She put her head on his shoulder. "Oh, Skip, I wanted to tell you. That first Sunday at the lake. Art dragged me outside and tried to kiss me."

"He what?" Skip almost drove the car off the road.

"He tried to kiss me," she sobbed. "I didn't tell you because I didn't want you to be upset. The debate was the next day. And then tonight was so strange. Donna told me she's going to break up with Art and that Art was acting weird. Then you were down in the boathouse with Art tonight, and when you came back you looked so pale and frightened. I don't know what to make of it. Everything is giving me the creeps tonight."

Skip gassed the station wagon, roaring toward Gaspee Farms, a quiet neighborhood with many Colonial-style houses. He didn't say a word until they got to Lisa's house.

"I'll talk to Art in the morning," he said.

"Skip, you aren't going to do anything tonight?" she asked pleadingly.

"Don't worry about me."

They kissed. Skip wiped a tear from her cheek. He was imagining the best way to get even with Art Lawing. Maybe Art would have a little surprise when he went out to Pine Island tomorrow morning to check on the scarf.

"Skip, promise me you won't—"

"I'll go straight home," he lied. "Call you in the morning."

Lisa got out of the car and walked slowly to her front door, turning to wave when Skip put the station wagon into gear and roared away.

Skip knew what he had to do. He put his hand in his coat pocket, pulling out the Cresswell High School scarf. Art was going to be the loser tomorrow morning when he went looking for the scarf in the basement of the Bigelow place. He just might have some trouble getting out of the basement, and then it would be Skip's turn to laugh.

Skip got back on the interstate and stopped at a convenience store for some candy bars to sustain him through the night ahead. Then he resumed driving until he saw the exit sign that read STORM LAKE, NORTH SHORE.

In a few minutes, his car rolled to a stop on the sandy shoulder of the dirt road on the north shore of the lake. Skip turned off the headlights and sat there for a moment. The sky had cleared overhead. A full harvest moon had appeared to illuminate the still night. He took the flashlight from the glove compartment and climbed out of the car.

The first nip of autumn chilled the air. Skip felt comfortable under his woolen coat. He had changed into warmer clothes before they went to the movie in Porterville.

"This is it," he muttered to himself.

Skip began to move cautiously on the side of the road. The entrance to the scout camp was just ahead of him. Skip had been there a dozen times. When he was younger, he had been a scout, rising to the rank of star scout. The camp was close to Pine Island, a great place to launch a boat or a canoe.

Skip saw the sign in the moonlight: OSWEGO SCOUT CAMP. A wooden beam blocked the entrance to the dirt road. Skip climbed over the gate and landed with a thud on the other side. Technically he was trespassing, but he figured that no one would fault a former scout for visiting his old haunts.

Trees loomed over him, blocking the moon as he started down the dirt road. Skip's breath fogged in the night air. There was almost no wind. The storm had left a calmness over the lake.

Skip stopped for a moment when he saw the caretaker's shack ahead of him. The scouts had held their fall jamboree on the previous weekend, and he was worried that the caretaker might still be around. He had to get past the cabin unnoticed.

Skip started forward, walking on his toes. There were no lights burning inside the cabin. He slipped by the cabin without making a sound. His plan was working perfectly—so far.

The ground began to slope downward toward the lake. Skip felt his way in the dark until he found the railing of the wooden stairs that led to the beach below. Stepping carefully down the stairs, he found his way to the flat stretch of sand.

Storm Lake was dead calm. The moon shimmered on the dark water. Skip walked along the beach until he came to an aluminum shape in the sand. The caretaker liked to fish, so he had not yet stored the last canoe for winter. Skip turned the canoe over to find a life jacket and a wooden paddle.

It was going to be easy. Art would have to eat his words, especially when Skip confronted him about his pass at Lisa. He was going to make Art suffer. He was certain of that.

Skip stepped into the canoe with one foot and pushed off from shore. He paddled gently and slowly. Pine Island was in the distance, about a half-mile away. The moon hung directly over the swelling mass of land. Skip could see the shape of the old Bigelow mansion against the sky. The back of his neck felt cold. The island was dark and foreboding. It seemed bigger at night. With the tree branches swaying in front of it, the old Bigelow house almost looked alive in the moonlight.

He remembered the scary story he had first heard around the campfire at the scout camp. In the early 1950s, old Farley Bigelow had, for no apparent reason, hacked his wife to death with a double-bladed ax. Some said that evil Indian spirits of the island had driven him to it. Others claimed that living with Mrs. Bigelow would have made anyone crazy. Whatever the reason for the murder, the head of the corpse had never been found. Old Man Bigelow had hidden it somewhere on the island.

Skip took the paddle out of the water for a moment. His mouth felt dry. His fears rose as he peered toward Pine Island. The sight of the house had spooked him. Some of his anger had begun to wear off. He started to wonder if maybe there was some other way to get even with Art.

But then he thought of Art trying to kiss Lisa. The image burned in his jealous mind. His courage soared again.

"I'll show him," he whispered, as if to a secret companion. "I'm going to do it."

Skip dug the paddle into the dark water. The canoe shot forward. A soft breeze rolled in from behind him. It pushed Skip toward Pine Island and the old house that awaited him.

Lisa saw Skip in the storm. The wind howled around him, throwing red and orange leaves in his face. Skip tried to fight the wind, but it kept pushing him back away from her.

Lisa reached out. She wanted to help him, but his own outstretched hands were receding. She called to him. Suddenly the wind formed a giant tornado on the lake. The tip of the cyclone snapped over Skip's head.

Skip rapidly disappeared. Lisa saw him flying into the sky. It was like something out of a movie.

An alarm began to ring somewhere. It sounded like a fire bell. Lisa heard someone calling her name.

"Lisa!"

Was it Skip?

"Lisa, wake up."

Her mother's voice roused Lisa from the nightmare. She sat up in bed. Her stomach felt queasy. The dream had seemed so real.

"Mom, what's wrong?"

"It's Mrs. Masters," her mother replied. "She's on the phone. She wants to talk to you."

Lisa looked at the clock. "But it's after one in the—Skip."

She got out of bed and hurried to the phone. "Mrs. Masters, this is Lisa. Is everything—Oh, no."

"What?" her mother asked.

Lisa put her hand over the mouthpiece. "Skip didn't come home yet."

"My word."

"Yes, Mrs. Masters, I'm still here. No, he dropped me off before midnight. He said he was heading straight home."

Mrs. Masters voiced her concerns at the other end of the line. Lisa wondered if she should tell everyone about the trouble with Art, but she decided against it for the time being. Maybe there was some innocent reason for his not returning home, such as a flat tire.

"Is everything all right?" her mother asked when Lisa got off the phone.

Lisa sighed. "I don't know. If he's not home in an hour, Mrs. Masters is going to call the police."

They went back to bed. Lisa couldn't sleep. She lay still for a long time, staring at the ceiling, wishing the bad feeling in her stomach would go away.

Chapter 10

Skip guided the canoe into a rocky cove. The moon was lost behind the pine trees that gave the island its name. Skip took out the flashlight and flashed its beam onto the shoreline.

"Wha—!"

A pair of luminous eyes stared back at Skip. He lost his breath for a moment. It seemed as though the head of Mrs. Bigelow had risen from the rocks.

There was a scuffling into the trees, and he saw a raccoon racing from the light. Skip filled his lungs and tried to shake the chill out of his shoulders.

Swinging the light upward, he studied the incline of the wooded area. Shiny, mica-filled rocks glittered between the trees. The rocks formed a path up the slope.

Suddenly Skip felt the exhilaration of the hunt. His heart was pumping, and adrenaline coursed through his body.

The bow of the canoe bumped against the shore. Skip climbed out and pulled the vessel onto the rocks. As he turned toward the path of stone, the flashlight flickered for a moment. He decided to save the batteries for the house, where he would need the light.

When the beam was gone, Skip stood still for a moment, letting his eyes adjust to the dull, purple darkness. He peered up into the trees. Many of the smaller maples had lost their leaves in the storm, leaving bare, skinny witch-fingers against the sky.

His nerves began to jangle again. At least he could see the path a little. His feet shuffled to the first rock step. Skip went up and walked a few more feet to the next tier. He had to get a better sense of where he was going.

Flashing the dim beam for a moment, he studied the lay of the land. With the image fresh in his mind, he started forward, success-fully rising on the trail. It was still slow going in the dark.

The path curved to the right. The house was visible above him, an imposing gothic castle on a hill.

Skip stopped and stared as a shape appeared momentarily in one of the windows of the dark house. But then the shape was gone and Skip figured it was just the remains of a curtain, flut-tering in the draft. He kept climbing toward the Bigelow manse.

The moon became bright as he broke out of

the trees. Skip picked up the pace, climbing higher toward the crest of the ridge.

When he reached the top of the walk, he peered toward the house. The old picket fence had rotted away to nothing. Broken windows let the rain and the wind into the dilapidated dwelling. The shutters that hadn't fallen off the clapboard were hanging by a nail, shifting and squeaking in the breeze.

For a moment, Skip thought about turning back. The old place was spooky. But then he heard Art calling him a chicken. He saw Bill laughing at him and telling everyone what a dweeb he had been.

He started toward the front stoop, driven by his urge for revenge against Art. Skip was a straight-up guy, not like Art, going around trying to kiss another guy's girlfriend.

Skip stopped when he reached the bottom of the stoop, and his eyes grew wide. He saw something he had not expected to find. He had anticipated that the biggest hassle of his task would be getting inside the Bigelow estate. But instead, he found that the door of the old place was wide open.

Skip's legs turned weak and wobbly. He thought about running right then. His eyes peered into the dark maw of the house. Why was the door open?

He put his foot on the first step. The board didn't collapse. When he shined the flickering light on the door, he saw that it had simply fallen off its hinges. A chill spread through his body. The breeze had begun to pick up. He swung the beam upward, piercing the deep shadows of the grim enclosure, and started into the house.

The floor creaked under Skip's weight. He took each step cautiously, feeling the boards in front of him. There were pieces of wood all around, as if someone had gone through the house with a crowbar, randomly smashing furniture and tearing up floorboards. In the middle of a run-down parlor, he stopped for a moment.

He had to find the basement.

Skip started to take another step. Something crashed in front of him, sliding down the wall. The sound of shattering glass echoed through the drafty rooms. Skip aimed the light at the window that had flown open. The wind was starting to blow hard again.

Through the open window, Skip could see the last traces of the moon. Dark clouds flowed from the north to smother the bright orb. Skip could hear thunder in the distance. An icy scale of harsh notes played up and down his spine. Another storm was brewing.

Droplets of rain began to pelt the house. Lightning streaked across the sky. Skip's body wanted to run. But his pride would not let him flee. He could hear Art's mocking laughter in the rumbling of the thunder.

He pushed on with the light, searching for the door to the basement.

A door flapped in the drafts of the old house. Skip felt a gust of wind on his face. He hurried to the doorway and wedged the door open. A flight of steps led downward into darkness. The first step was sound. He took the steps carefully, one at a time, finding his way in the orange wash of the dimming flashlight.

Skip saw water at the bottom of the stairs. The basement had been flooded by the rains. Then something splashed in the water. He turned the weak light on something that looked like a rodent, swimming toward the opposite wall.

The basement water was thick and murky. A fetid stench stung his eyes and nostrils. He blinked as he found his way to the bottom step, the last one before the water. When he swung the light into the basement, he forgot about everything except the scarf that he unwrapped from his neck. All he had to do was affix the scarf to the beam in the center of the basement and wait out the night. When Art came over in the morning to see if he had hung the scarf, Skip would wedge some of the wood against the door and trap him in the basement. Then he would decide how to play with Art's mind after that.

Skip stepped down into the wet ooze of the basement floor. The water crept up to his thighs. Something slithered out from under his feet, but Skip didn't stop for a moment. He moved straight for the rafter.

The broad wooden beam was only a couple of feet over his head. Skip saw a nail protruding from the beam. He could hang the scarf there. It would be good enough. As he reached upward, the flashlight's beam flickered and died.

He was lost in the darkness. Somewhere in a wet corner of the basement, the rodent was scurrying to reclaim its territory. His fingers ran along the beam until he found the nail. He put the scarf in place and started back toward the stairs.

His legs sloshed in the dirty water. He knew the stairs were in front of him. He just had to find them.

Skip almost fell into the water when he saw a bright shaft of light flashing in the stairwell. At first he thought it was a reflection of the spectral lightning. Then he realized it was a flashlight!

"Who's there?" Skip called in an unsteady voice.

Footsteps rattled the staircase. Suddenly the light turned to flash in his eyes. It was an intense, blinding beam. He couldn't see the intruder, but he was almost sure that it was Art behind the beam.

"Get that thing out of my face, Lawing!" Skip cried.

A voice slithered out of a speaker. "Resolved: You're dead."

"I've had enough of this," Skip shouted.

Now there was music in the basement. Apparently the intruder had brought a radio with him. Skip couldn't see that the radio was attached to a long, orange electrical cord that carried two hundred and twenty volts of live current.

"Give it up, Lawing!"

No reply beyond the sound of a DJ's glib chatter on the radio. "It's two A.M. at WCRS, home of Cresswell's hottest hits. Now, kicking off a solid hour of recent oldies, here's Eddie Grant, gonna rock on over to 'Electric Avenue.'"

Something fell through the light. The radio hit the water. Skip suddenly felt the voltage as it flowed through him.

"No!"

His body shook as the current told hold, biting deep into him. He twitched in the watery slime of the Bigelow basement. The electricity seared his flesh. He died quickly.

Chapter 11

Lisa couldn't take it any longer. She had been staring at the ceiling for nearly two hours, unable to sleep. She climbed out of bed, dressed quickly, and hurried into the living room. Then she wrote a note and left it on the lampshade for her mother.

Stepping out the front door, Lisa emerged into the stormy night. The tempest still raged over Cresswell. Lisa stared up the street, wondering if she should attempt the journey in the storm.

Pulling her overcoat tightly around her, she finally started forward against the wind. Walking in the storm was better than tossing and turning all night. She hurried along the sidewalk as thunder and lightning filled the clouded sky. But Lisa kept going even as the heavy rain crashed down upon her.

Lisa couldn't shake the anxious feeling that had crept over her, keeping her awake. The dreamlike image of Skip being swallowed by the storm wouldn't leave her. She was trudging the ten blocks to his house, nursing the hope that she would see the station wagon in the driveway when she arrived. But only the Oldsmobile that Mr. Masters drove was there as she approached the house.

The lights were on in the living room. Her heart pounding in her chest, Lisa hurried up the walk. She knocked loudly. The door opened a few seconds later. Lisa could see the worry in Mrs. Masters's face.

"Lisa, what are you—"

"I'm sorry to bother you, Mrs. Masters. But I was worried about Skip. Did he ever come home?"

Mrs. Masters shook her head. "No. But don't apologize, Lisa. We're worried, too. Come on in out of the rain."

As Mrs. Masters ushered her inside, the phone began to ring. Mr. Masters was also awake. Lisa froze, anticipating bad news as he lifted the receiver. It was Lisa's mother, wanting to know if Lisa was there.

Lisa took the receiver from Mr. Masters. "I'm okay, Mom. I know I shouldn't have come out in the rain, but I was worried about Skip. No, I didn't wake them, they were already up."

Mr. Masters leaned closer to Lisa. "Tell her I'll bring you home. I want to keep the line open."

"I have to go, Mom. No, Mr. Masters says he'll give me a ride home. I have to hang up, he wants to keep the line open. Okay, Mom. I know. I'm sorry. I'll be home soon."

She hung up.

"Have you called the sheriff yet?" Lisa asked.

Mr. Masters sighed. "We tried, but the lines have been busy. There's a bridge out down at River Point. Do you think Skip went down there?"

Lisa felt chill bumps on her arms. "No, he said he was coming straight home. But there was some trouble, Mr. Masters, between him and Art."

"We called Art's house," Mrs. Masters replied. "But he hadn't seen Skip since he left the party with you and Donna."

Mr. Masters picked up the phone again. "I'm going to try the sheriff one more time. There, it's ringing."

"The lines should be clear," Mrs. Masters said. "It's almost three A.M."

Lisa kept waiting to hear that Skip had only been delayed by car trouble. She wanted to put her arms around him and feel him next to her. But the thunder only made it worse.

"Pick up the phone," Mr. Masters said under his breath. "If you—Yes! My name is Masters. I'd like to report a missing person. . . ."

Chapter 12

By morning, the skies over Storm Lake were no longer dumping rain on the Lawing house. A heavy cloud cover still hung low in the valley, but the bad part of the storm had passed. The waters of the lake were smooth and clear once again. Birds circled in the air currents and chipmunks foraged on the shoreline, readying themselves for the threat of the approaching winter.

Art Lawing opened his eyes and looked at the time on his clock radio. It was seven A.M. He jumped out of bed and hurried to the window. Dawn had broken, but Pine Island was only a blurred hump in the distance. A strange smile spread over Art's handsome face. He dressed quickly and started downstairs.

His mother and father were still in bed. It was just as well. Art had a task to perform, and he wanted to get it over with. He had plans for the rest of the day.

After stepping out of the house, Art walked carefully across the wet lawn. He still had to clean up the outdoor mess from the party that had been ruined by the rain. Paper plates and napkins dotted the grass beside the red and gold leaves that had fallen in the wake of the tempest.

"Disaster city," he muttered to himself.

Art headed for the boathouse. The flat lake was perfect for a ride in the speedboat. When he reached the end of the grass, he stopped suddenly. The door to the boathouse was ajar. Had it blown open during the storm? Art had remembered locking it after he and Bill were finished with Skip.

Cautiously, he stepped onto the dock, easing toward the open door. He stopped, peering into the shadows. Someone was moving around inside. Art slipped through the doorway, grabbing an oar that leaned against the wall. He held the oar in front of him as he studied the obscure shape in the shadows. Someone was standing next to the boat.

He called into the darkness. "Bill?"

"No, it's me."

Donna stepped away from the boat. She was dressed in jeans and a heavy canvas raincoat. She looked unhappy.

Art let out a deep breath. "Donna, you scared me. What are you doing here, anyway?"

She sighed, lowering her head. "I had to talk to you. I couldn't sleep all night."

Art made a scoffing sound as he put the oar

back where he had found it. "Talk to me, huh? You didn't want to talk to me yesterday when you ran off before the party was over."

"I know," she replied. "That's what I'm talking about. We need to communicate, Art."

"So you come out here at seven o'clock on Sunday morning?"

"I had to talk to you. I told you, I couldn't sleep all night. I came out early, but when I saw no one was awake, I parked my car on the road and walked back here. I wanted to wait until someone got up."

"What's with you?" Art asked bluntly. "First you desert me at the party yesterday, and now I find you lurking around the boathouse at seven o'clock the next morning."

"I'm sorry, Art. I didn't feel well yesterday."

"Oh, yeah? Didn't feel well. That's lame, Donna. If you didn't feel well, why did you go down to Porterville with Skip and Lisa?"

"Art, please."

Art wasn't going to let her off the hook easily. "Maybe you've got the hots for Skip. You want to take the sophomore away from his girlfriend!"

"Get off it," Donna replied. "I went with them because I got tired of you and those obnoxious country-club brats. They were acting like children. I don't even know why you invited them."

Art frowned at her. "Chill out, Donna. I just

75

thought it might liven up the party. If it bothered you so much, you should have said something."

"I did say something," Donna replied. "But you never listen. You just go on and do whatever you want. Look, Art, I don't know how to say this, but . . ."

He moved toward her, putting his fingers on her lips. "Hey, let's not fight. I forgive you for leaving the party. It's no big thing."

Donna chortled incredulously. *"You* forgive *me?"*

"I don't want everyone to be mad at me," Art replied. "Mom is plenty ticked about the party. After you left, things got out of hand a little. It took me almost till midnight to clean up after those dweebs. And you're right, they are jerks. I hope I never see them again."

Donna squinted at Art, eyeing him in the dim light of the boathouse.

"Give me a break, Donna. Hey, I'm sorry."

"Art, I—"

He turned away, jumping into the boat. "Look, I was just getting ready to go for a ride. Let's take her out."

"I don't think so," Donna replied. "Art, I have to talk to you. It's very important."

He waved at her. "Come on, we can talk on the water."

"Art, *please.*"

"Hey, if you want to talk to me, you have to

76

come along. Otherwise, you can wait until I get back."

"All right!"

Donna reluctantly boarded the boat. Art cleared the lines and pushed the boat away from the dock. Donna had to help him lift the big doors that opened onto the lake. The boat floated out into the cove in front of his house.

"Not so bad, is it?" Art asked.

Donna ignored him.

As the vessel drifted away from the shoreline, Donna sat in the passenger seat and folded her arms. Art moved behind the steering wheel. Donna did not want to go for a ride, but she had to humor him for the moment.

"Huh," Art said, "that's strange."

Donna sighed impatiently. "What now?"

"I thought the gas tank was full," he replied, "but it's half empty. The needle must've been stuck."

"I don't want to talk about gas gauges," Donna said curtly.

"Oh, yeah. Well, what do you want to talk about?"

She turned to glare at him. "I'd like to discuss that pass you made at Lisa a couple of weeks ago. You tried to kiss her by the lake."

Art grimaced. "She ratted me out!"

"No, I saw it all from the kitchen window."

Art turned the key in the ignition. The outboard engine roared to life, drowning her out.

He kept revving the motor so Donna couldn't be heard. The echo rolled over the still lake.

"Stop it, Art!"

He started to put the boat in gear. Donna jumped up quickly and turned off the engine. Art tried to get the key from her, but Donna put it inside her raincoat.

"I could have a good time trying to get that away from you," Art said. "A full body search. Mind if I try?" He leaned toward her.

Donna pushed him back. "Yes, I do mind!"

"Lighten up."

"Art, don't you ever think about anyone but yourself?"

He threw out his hands. "What's your problem? You're the one who left the party. You're the one who showed up first thing in the morning with all this grief!"

Donna shook her head. "It's hopeless, Art. It's just hopeless."

She looked away, staring out over Storm Lake. She was trying to find the words to make their breakup final. But before she could speak, something else caught her attention in the distance.

"What's that?" Donna said, pointing toward Pine Island.

Art saw it, too. A rotating blue light flashed near the eastern shore of the island. There seemed to be some sort of emergency in the deeper water.

Donna looked at him. "What . . ."

Art's face turned pale as he shook his head. "I don't know. I didn't see it this morning. Give me back the key and we'll go have a look."

Donna handed him the key to the boat's ignition. He started the outboard again. Donna held on tightly as the boat took off, planing on the smooth surface of Storm Lake. They headed rapidly toward Pine Island and the flashing blue light that reflected on the water.

Art stared straight ahead, steering toward the two outboard-powered vessels that were moving off Pine Island. When Art and Donna drew closer, they could see that the boats were official. One of them belonged to the marine patrol; the other bore the insignia of the sheriff's department.

Art eased back on the throttle. He took the boat out of gear, idling as he watched the other vessels. His heart was pounding. He knew there was going to be trouble. A deputy sheriff was reaching over the side of one of the boats into the lake.

Donna stood up so she could see better. "I wonder what happened."

Art shook his head. Sweat dripped off him in the cool, misty air of Storm Lake.

"Are you all right, Art?"

"Yeah, fine."

Donna looked toward the other boats again. They had stopped. Suddenly the sheriff's deputy turned to wave at them. He beckoned them toward his boat.

"He wants us to come over," Donna said.

But Art didn't move right away. He kept staring at the man in the khaki uniform. The deputy waved again. Art's knuckles turned white on the steering wheel. He was afraid of what the deputy had found in the water.

"We better do as he says," Donna offered. "Art?"

"Yeah, all right."

Art shifted the engine into forward gear. The boat surged toward the police craft. The marine patrol boat was on the other side of the deputy sheriff's. Donna thought the officers were fishing for something in the water. While one officer steered the vessel, the other one stabbed at something with a sharp gaffe, as if he was trying to land a trout.

As they drew closer to the deputy sheriff, Art eased back on the throttle. He shifted into neutral, coasting toward the man in the uniform. The deputy caught the bow of the boat. He steadied it alongside the official craft.

"Good morning, officer," Art said. A slight, friendly smirk stretched across his face.

"What are you two doing out so early?" the deputy asked, peering at them with narrow eyes.

Art shrugged. "Just wanted to get in one more run before we put the boat up for the winter. You know, empty the gas tank before the lake freezes."

Donna asked the deputy what had happened.

"There's been an accident."

"Anything we can do to help?" Art asked.

The officer studied Art with his narrow eyes. "What's your name, son?"

"Lawing, sir. Art Lawing."

"And you, young lady?"

"Donna Forsi."

The deputy nodded toward Art. "Doesn't your father own Lawing Construction?"

"Yes, sir."

"You're sweating, Art. Are you hot?"

Art wiped his forehead with the back of his hand. "Yeah. I came from my morning run and went straight to the boathouse."

"Is that right, Miss Forsi?"

Donna frowned at the deputy. "I don't know. I was waiting in the boathouse when he got there."

The deputy sighed. "If you don't mind, I'd like you kids to answer a few questions for me."

"Hey, anything," Art said, fawning a little. He could feel Donna's skeptical eyes upon him.

The deputy glanced over his shoulder toward a canoe tied up to the marine vessel. "Either one of you ever see that canoe before?"

Art shook his head. "No."

"I've never seen it," Donna rejoined.

"We think it came from the scout camp," the deputy went on. "Art, did you have some kind of party yesterday?"

"Uh, yes, I did. But the rain trashed it. After the storm was over, my mom sent everyone home."

Art wondered how the deputy knew about the party. Maybe he had been on patrol the day before and had seen Art's driveway full of cars.

"Is that right, Miss Forsi? Art's mother sent everyone home?"

Donna's brow wrinkled. "I guess so."

"What kind of answer is that?"

Art held his breath, wondering what she would say. Donna usually told the truth. She was too honest sometimes.

"I left the party a little early," Donna replied. "I went down to Porterville with my friends Lisa and Skip."

The deputy winced. "Skip Masters?"

"Yes, how did you know?"

The deputy pulled a waterlogged wallet out of his jacket. "Is this him?" He showed them the picture on Skip's driver's license.

Donna's face went slack. "Yes. What's happened to him?"

"We think he took the canoe from the scout camp."

Donna peered toward the marine patrol boat. "Where is he?"

"Did you know him?" the officer asked.

"Yes, sir," Art answered. "We're all on the debating team at Cresswell. I hope Skip is all right."

Then Donna, who had been observing the efforts of the marine officers, suddenly let out a scream. "No!"

The marine officers were pulling the body from the lake. Donna recognized the jacket that Skip had been wearing the night before. She put her hands over her face and sunk down into the boat's seat. Art put his trembling arm around her shoulder.

"We found his car up by the entrance of the scout camp about five o'clock this morning," the officer went on. "His father called us about three. When we couldn't find him up at the scout camp, we came down to the lake. The canoe was floating across the water."

Art and Donna stared silently as the lifeless body was hoisted into the marine patrol boat.

"Do either of you know why he would be on the lake in the middle of the night?" the officer asked.

"No," Art said.

The deputy turned toward Donna, who still sobbed into her hands. "I'm sorry, Miss Forsi. Didn't you say you were with him last night?"

She nodded.

"Did he give any indication of why he might be coming out to this lake? Any reason why he'd take that canoe?"

She shook her head.

The deputy looked at Art. "How 'bout it, Lawing? Any clue as to why he would come out here?"

"He used to be a boy scout," Art replied. "But no, I have no idea why he was out here."

They were quiet for a moment. The deputy turned to watch as the marine officers wrapped the body in a canvas tarp. When the corpse was covered, the marine officers waved at the deputy. They started their boat and headed back toward the scout camp. An ambulance sat waiting on the shore.

"Did Skip drown?" Donna asked.

The deputy exhaled tiredly. "Looks like he was struck by lightning."

"Lightning?" Art said. "Tough way to go."

"Oh, shut up," Donna snapped. "Don't talk about Skip like that."

"Sorry," Art replied.

Donna glanced up at the deputy. "Have you told his parents yet?"

"No," the officer replied blankly. "We just found the body. But I'll call them when I get back to shore."

"I have to tell his girlfriend," Donna said. "Lisa and I are best friends."

The deputy took out a pad and a pencil. "What's her name?"

"Lisa," Art replied quickly. "Lisa Enright."

The officer wrote down the name. "Okay, kids. Thanks. I'm sorry you had to see this."

"So am I," Donna muttered.

Art sighed. "It's okay, officer."

"Look," the deputy said, "I may want to talk to you again."

"Any time," Art replied. "Skip was our friend."

The deputy started the boat and headed toward the scout camp. Art frowned at the shore. He felt a churning in his gut. He wondered if he had been cool enough. He surely didn't want anyone to find out that he had goaded Skip into pulling the ridiculous stunt.

"Take me back to your house," Donna said.

"Sure."

As Art turned his head, he caught a glimpse of Pine Island. The mound of rock rose right there in front of them. The deputy hadn't even mentioned the Bigelow house, which was barely visible between the trees. Skip had been found floating in the lake. There was no connection.

"Art! Get going. I want to get back to town."

"Right."

Art threw the boat into gear, turning away from Pine Island. The speedboat roared back across the water, toward the Lawing house. A slight breeze had stirred the lake into a chop. Donna held on tightly to the safety grip.

When the bow of the boat touched the dock,

Donna jumped out and left without saying a word to Art. She ran down the dock and across the yard. She found her car on the shoulder of the road, where she had left it earlier that morning. It was actually her father's car. Donna had told him that she was coming out to Art's to get something she had left behind the night before.

In a trance, she drove back to Cresswell. Her heart was pounding as she turned onto the street where Skip had lived. *Had* lived! He was really gone. She had seen the body coming out of the lake. She could still hear his voice.

She stopped in front of the Masters' place. They had probably just received the news. The tears came back. She couldn't control them for a while. She had to compose herself before she got out of the car.

The front door opened as Donna clomped up the steps. She was surprised to see Lisa come out onto the porch. Lisa's brown eyes were red from crying. Donna's whole body felt weak.

They embraced, both of them crying.

From inside the house, they could hear the loud, anguished sobbing of Mrs. Masters.

Chapter 13

Jeffrey Goodman was not an early riser by nature. He hated getting up for school on weekdays, so on Saturday and Sunday he liked to sleep as late as possible. He would languish in adolescent dreams, warmed by reveries that he could never repeat to anyone. For Jeffrey, waking was always more frightening than any nightmare he might have during his slumber.

When his eyes opened, Jeffrey glared at the blurry window in front of him. He reached for his glasses, trying to bring a hostile world into focus. Every day Jeffrey was reminded that he was a dweeb, a bookworm, an egghead, a kid from the Basin who just happened to be smart. He would never score a touchdown or even make the team. He would never win the ten-thousand-dollar debating scholarship. It would go to someone, like Art, who didn't even need the money.

Jeffrey rolled out of bed, putting his feet on

the floor. His foot hit something. Jeffrey looked at the catalogue from Fillmore Community College. His mother had brought it home for him. Jeffrey figured he would qualify for some rinky-dink financial aid, but he would never be able to attend a really first-rate university.

Standing, he found his robe and pulled it on. As he was leaving his room, he absently switched on the small portable television his mother had given him for his birthday. He then traipsed down the hall to the bathroom.

When he came back into his room, Jeffrey flopped back on the bed wishing he could go to sleep again. He was half listening to the sound from the television. A special bulletin had interrupted regular programming. The name of the dead person caught Jeffrey's ear.

. . . *was identifed as Skip Masters of Cresswell* . . .

Jeffrey sat up in his bed. He saw Skip's face looming at him from the screen. The station had pulled the picture from the yearbook. The visual image switched to a still slide of Storm Lake.

. . . *Masters, a sophomore member of the debating team, was found dead in Storm Lake about five hours after his parents reported that he had not come home from a date.* . . .

Jeffrey stared at the screen. Skip was dead. His picture flashed again behind the voice-over.

. . . believed to have been struck by light-ning . . .

Art and Bill had been planning something for the sophomore.

. . . a canoe stolen from the boy scout camp where Skip Masters had once been a happy camper . . .

Jeffrey shook his head, squinting at the screen. A strange smirk had come over his face. He almost looked happy.

. . . has not yet determined why Skip Masters was in the canoe on the storm-tossed waters of the lake . . .

"Incredible," Jeffrey whispered. "What have you done? What *have* you done?"

After tying up the boat, Art raced to his room and called Bill. He prayed for Bill to pick up the phone, so he wouldn't have to offer any explanations to Mr. or Mrs. Boland for calling so early.

"Hello."

"Bill, it's me. Art."

"Oh, hi."

"I've got some news for you," said Art. "Hang on. Skip was found dead this morning on Storm Lake."

Bill let out a whistle. "Incredible," he exclaimed. "How did you find out?"

"Donna and I saw the police lights out near

Pine Island, so we took the boat over to see what was going on."

"Donna? What was she doing there?"

"She came by this morning to talk to me. I had to take her out in the boat."

"Why?"

"She was waiting for me in the boathouse," Art said. "I couldn't just tell her to get lost."

"Does she know about the hazing, Art?"

Art's voice cracked a little. "Not on the phone, man. I don't want to talk about this over the phone."

"Listen to me, Art. We aren't going to tell anyone about what happened. Do you hear me?"

"What if they figure it out?" Art asked.

"They won't," Bill offered. "Besides, we didn't do anything. Not really."

"I'm not saying a word, Boland. I swear. Not a word."

"Good man."

"It wouldn't do anything but hurt us," Art went on. "I never thought he'd be stupid enough to go. Did you?"

Bill said nothing on the other end of the line.

Art whistled through his teeth. "Struck by lightning. That's a tough way to go. Can you believe it? Boland?"

"Gotta go," Bill said suddenly. "My father wants to use the phone. Later, Art."

"Cool. I won't say a word."

"Me neither."

Art hung up the phone. Climbing off his bed, he stepped to the window and peered out toward Storm Lake. He could see Pine Island resting under the clouds. The old Bigelow estate hid in the shadows, threatening to reveal all its secrets.

Donna guided her father's car down the rain-washed street. Lisa sat on the other side of the seat with her head hung. She looked spent, completely limp and wasted.

Lisa had been crying for a long time. Donna had taken her quickly from the Masters' household. For a while, they had been driving around aimlessly.

Donna stopped the car in front of Lisa's house. "You're home."

"Thank you," Lisa said weakly. "Thank you for bringing me home."

Donna looked away with tears forming in her eyes. "I'm sorry about Skip."

"What happened?" Lisa asked desperately. "Why was he out on that lake in a scout canoe? Was it because I told him that Art tried to kiss me? I don't understand, Donna."

They sat for a moment quietly.

"I had better go in," Lisa said at last.

They embraced again. Lisa got out of the car. She walked to the door without looking back.

Donna dried her eyes. She would stand beside Lisa at Skip's funeral. After that, they would grow apart for a while. They would not be close again until the real trouble started about seven weeks later at Christmastime.

Chapter 14

Bill Boland was ready for Christmas vacation. The fall semester had seemed to go on forever. He was exhausted, and his head always seemed to be aching. He would be walking in the hall or standing at his locker when the ice-skate blade split the top of his head. The pain was too much. Bill couldn't endure another day at Cresswell High.

When the last bell rang, Bill hurried out of his chemistry class. He wanted to get the rest of his books from his locker and head home. Maybe then his head would stop hurting.

Bill was halfway to his locker when he saw her. Lisa turned the corner. She was heading for the stairs. Bill smiled, but she did not even see him. Lisa went down the stairwell, disappearing on the floor below.

Her name formed on his lips. Always Lisa. Bill still loved her, even if she would not look his way. She was so beautiful. There had to be a way to get to her.

"Hey, Boland!"

Jeffrey Goodman stepped up next to him.

"Hi, Jeffrey."

"Still bumming over Lisa?" Jeffrey asked.

Bill glanced sideways at him. "Forget it."

"Hey, I'm on your side," Jeffrey replied. "Have you seen Art?"

"No."

"Want to go for pizza?" Jeffrey asked. "Celebrate three weeks of freedom?"

"No, I'm going home."

Jeffrey smiled. "Some year, huh? Funny how it all worked out. I mean, I'm on the team. It was a shame about Skip."

Bill looked away. "Yeah, a shame."

"The team is shaping up," Jeffrey went on proudly. "I can't wait till the spring debates. I mean, we're two and two counting that win at Marshfield. We'll still have a chance for the state title. I think Mr. Ferris is considering me for that scholarship."

Bill shook his head. "Nah, it'll go to Art or Donna. Probably Art."

"I could win!" Jeffrey said.

"Sure, Jeffrey."

Bill stomped off down the hall. His head was hurting so badly that he could barely see the numbers on the dial of the combination lock. When he opened the door to his locker, something fell out onto the floor. It was a piece of yellow construction paper that had been folded and slipped through the air vent of the locker.

Bill picked up the paper and unfolded it. His eyes grew wide. Written in big block letters were the words RESOLVED: BILL BOLAND KILLED SKIP!

In his mind, Bill saw the events of that night as if he were watching a home video. After the party at Art's, he had decided to kill Skip. When the lights went out in Art's house, Bill had sneaked back to borrow the speedboat. He took the boat to the north end of the lake, on the other side of Pine Island.

As he climbed to the top of the hill through the dark woods, Bill was thinking about clubbing Skip to death. His plans had changed when he almost ran into the power pole.

The pole rested below the Bigelow estate. Someone from the mainland was ready to begin development in the woods. They had already installed a live electric pole for the well. There was plenty of wire stacked high around the power pole. But even then the notion of electrocution didn't strike him at the time.

Bill had gone on, trekking to the old mansion in the darkness. When he was inside, he saw the water on the basement floor. His plan depended on Skip's having the courage to come all the way to the island. He felt confident that Skip was angry enough and egotistical enough to go through with it. If Skip made it into the basement, Bill knew he would have no trouble shocking him to death.

As he drove home, Bill thought of the way he had rigged the wire to run into the Bigelow house. The radio had been in the boat from the hazing earlier that evening. He could still see Skip jumping about in the knee-deep water.

After Skip was gone, Bill had unhooked the electrical cords. He fished the radio out of the water and then returned the wires to the power pole. No one had mentioned the wires, and Art had not missed the radio. Art would never miss the radio.

Bill turned off an exit that led into town. He remembered how easy it had been when the wires were in place. After returning to the mansion, he dragged Skip's body down to the Lawings' speedboat. He eased the craft around to the southern end of the island. He swamped the canoe and then dumped Skip overboard. He went back to the Lawings', slipped the boat into the boathouse, and hurried home in the middle of the night.

No one had suspected him of a thing. He could not believe the coroner's report—death by lightning. He had been in the clear until the strange note appeared in his locker.

RESOLVED: BILL BOLAND KILLED SKIP.

Chapter 15

A light, dusty snow fell over Cresswell. Winter had arrived, bringing with it the promise of a white Christmas. Multicolored lights and tinsel garlands festooned Warren Street, turning the sidewalk into an ideal scene from a holiday greeting-card picture. The sprinkling of snow caught the light from the storefronts, rendering Cresswell all the more appealing to shoppers who scurried about with only three more days left to buy gifts.

Lisa Enright was unaffected by the joy of the season that enlivened the whole town. She moved slowly along Warren Street, dragging her boots in the thin layer of slush. Her pale cheeks had been reddened by the chill. But Lisa didn't really feel the cold that surrounded her.

As she moved along the street, Lisa kept looking back over her shoulder, watching for the bus. She was still three blocks away from the bus stop where she could catch the bus that would take her to the cemetery. She picked up her pace when a bus suddenly rushed past. There would not be another one for an hour.

The bus was waiting when Lisa arrived. The door closed suddenly. Lisa ran to the curb, banging on the door until the driver opened it and let her in. She dropped the coins into the fare box and took a seat beside one of the gray windows.

Lisa fell into the trance that had settled on her since Skip's death. Her grief had lessened, but the gnawing darkness still plagued her spirits. She had even turned down her parents' offer to take her to Colorado over the Christmas break. Lisa could not enjoy a ski trip with the thorn of gloom lodged deep in her heart.

Skip was always there with her, living in her memory. She looked at the gold locket that Skip had given to her. There was an inscription on the inside cover: *To L.E. Love S.M.* Lisa held the locket to her heart and then put it away.

The bus hissed and screeched to a grinding halt. Lisa looked up quickly. She did not want to miss her stop. It was a long way to her final destination. The bus hadn't even reached the halfway mark.

Lisa sank back into her seat. Since Skip's death, she had been sleepwalking through her life. Nothing really seemed to matter. She had even quit as the secretary of the debating team. It was too painful to watch Jeffrey Goodman try to fill Skip's shoes.

As the bus passed All Saints' Church, Lisa heard the bells pealing the hour. It was only four o'clock, but evening shadows had already grown long over the city. The dim winter light didn't help her spirits any.

As the bus turned onto Congress Road, heading away from Cresswell Center, Lisa watched the landscape she had seen so many times on the journeys since Skip's funeral. The bus always dropped her off right in front of the cemetery where Skip was buried.

Marble and granite markers stretched over the rolling mound of land that had been a cemetery since 1781. It seemed to Lisa like a lonely place for Skip to be resting.

Lisa's boots crunched in the layer of undisturbed snow that covered the graveyard, as she walked straight to Skip's gravestone. Except for the brown-eyed, somber girl, the cemetery was deserted. On an evergreen limb near the equipment shack, a few birds fought for position on a suet bag. Lisa did not even hear their chirping protests.

His full name was on the marker: *Arnold David "Skip" Masters.* Beneath the dates of his birth and death were the words *Taken too soon.* A trumpeter angel looked down over the grave from the top of the stone.

"I'm here," Lisa said softly.

She just stood there silently with her brown eyes fixed on the ground. Lisa always came to the cemetery with a sense of expectation, but the feeling vanished as soon as she looked down at the grave. Skip was not going to rise out of the earth. The trumpeter angel would never sound the fanfare to bring him back to life.

Lisa sighed. She had stopped asking why Skip had been taken from her. Even the trips to his grave were becoming tiresome. And yet, she could not stop herself from taking the bus ride every time she was able to get away from town. It was a well-worn habit.

"I don't know what to do, Skip."

Something moved behind her. A dark figure stepped out from behind the snow-tipped evergreens.

Lisa felt panic surging inside her. Her arms and legs had grown numb from fear and the cold. She wanted to run, but a stiffness froze her chest.

Lisa looked back over her shoulder. "Don't come near me!"

"No! Stay! Lisa, it's me!"

Donna's face emerged from the darkness. Lisa began to cry. Donna put her arms around her shoulders. She led Lisa toward the iron gate. Her father's car was parked on the other side of Congress Road. Lisa had settled down by the time they were inside the warm sedan.

"How did you find me out here?" Lisa asked blankly.

Donna shrugged. "Just lucky."

But the whole school knew about Lisa's frequent visits to Skip's grave. One ridiculous rumor had Lisa going mad and trying to dig up the body. Others speculated that Lisa's excessive grief stemmed from her part in Skip's mysterious demise.

"Haven't seen you around much," Donna said. "Since you quit the debating team, we haven't even been able to find a new secretary."

Lisa sighed. "You got me onto the team, Donna. I hope I haven't let you down. I hope I didn't hurt the team."

"No," Donna said. "We just miss you. And the team hasn't done too badly. We lost twice, but we did have that win at Marshfield. We're two and two."

"I just can't bear to watch Jeffrey up there."

"I'm worried about you, Lisa," Donna said bluntly. "Everyone is worried about you."

"I'm okay," Lisa replied softly, looking away.

"No, you're not. You haven't been able to snap out of it. You don't seem to care about anything. Your grades have fallen, and you don't pay attention in your classes."

Lisa looked back to scowl angrily at her. "What do you know!"

"Look at you!" Donna cried. "What is it, Lisa? Why can't you accept what happened? Tell me!"

Tears rolled out of her eyes. "I don't know,

Donna. It's not right. Something is just not right. Nobody knows what really happened to Skip."

Donna gave a deep, exasperated sigh. "I know, Lisa. I know. But now I think I have a few ideas."

She put the car into gear and headed back to Cresswell. Lisa gaped at her. There was a strange edge in Donna's voice. The sandy-haired girl had a serious expression on her pretty face.

"What are you talking about, Donna?"

"Nobody can figure out why Skip was on Storm Lake," Donna replied. "Even the sheriff came up empty. Everything was fine that evening. We had a good time at the movies—"

"Then I told Skip about Art trying to kiss me," Lisa interjected.

Donna laughed. "Art. Hah."

"What about Art?" Lisa asked.

Donna stopped the car on the shoulder of the road. "Listen to me, Lisa. Do you want to keep moping around? Or do you want to find out why Skip really died on Storm Lake?"

"Donna, what can we do about it?"

She leaned back with her hands on the wheel. "I'm not sure, Lisa. That day, before we went down to Porterville, Skip was down in the boathouse with some guys. Maybe it was Art and Bill."

"What about Jeffrey?"

"Okay, he might have been there, too," Donna said. "The point is, Skip wasn't in that boathouse alone."

"I know," said Lisa. "And I remember that he seemed strange when he came back into the kitchen. But when I stop to think about it, he was no stranger than when we first arrived. He didn't really want to go to the party."

"Did Skip like Art and Bill?" Donna asked quickly.

"No, not really."

"I keep replaying the day in my mind," Donna went on. "I can't think of anything that might have made Skip go out on the lake in that canoe. He seemed strange to me, too, when he came out of that boathouse. He was sort of pale."

"Donna, do you think—?"

Donna finished the question. "That something happened in the boathouse to make Skip want to take that canoe and go out onto the lake?"

A sudden expression of recognition spread over Lisa's face. "Yes! That was the only time I wasn't with him. He was down there with the others. But Art and Bill never said anything to the sheriff."

Donna threw out her hands. "I rest my case, Perry Mason. Besides you and me, they were the last ones to see Skip before he died."

"*If* they were the ones in the boathouse," Lisa challenged.

"I'm saying they were."

Lisa frowned. "Then why didn't they mention that to the sheriff?"

"Probably to keep from getting in trouble."

Lisa exhaled, shaking her head slowly. "I don't know, Donna. You're still on the debating team. Has Art been any different?"

"He's been colder," Donna replied. "I did break up with him. But on the day they found Skip . . . I mean, that day on the lake, he was acting strange. It was almost like he was expecting something bad to happen. I just keep remembering the look on his face."

"Why would they do something to hurt Skip?"

"Art didn't like him," Donna replied. "Neither did Bill. He took Jeffrey's place on the team, so Jeffrey didn't like Skip."

"But would they kill him?"

Donna grimaced. "No, I don't think anything like that. I just think they know why Skip was on that lake."

Lisa sat up straight. "All right. How do we find out what they know?"

Donna looked sideways at her. "Are you really ready to help me?"

"Yes," Lisa replied, "but where do we start?"

Donna put the car into gear, steering through the deep shadows of twilight. "We'll start at my house," she replied. "I've already made some notes. We've got the whole Christmas break to figure something out."

Lisa's posture had changed. She was no longer hunched over and depressed. Her brown eyes had come back to life. And the feeling of anticipation had returned, filling her with a vague but warming hope.

Just ten minutes later, when they were two blocks from Donna's house, they were surprised to see Bill Boland's lanky frame swaying down the sidewalk. His hands were in the pockets of a long coat.

"What's he doing in my neighborhood at this time of day?" Donna said.

"Doesn't he live in Rocky Bank Estates?" Lisa asked.

"Yes."

"Follow him," Lisa urged. "See what he does."

"Okay."

Bill continued to stride through the slush. Flurries still whirled in the air, even if they did not stick on the sidewalk. Donna held back, letting Bill stay a half-block ahead of them. Bill finally turned onto the side street. Donna accelerated, rounding the corner in time to see Bill disappearing into an alley that served as the driveway for Donna's house.

"He's sneaking around behind your place!" Lisa cried.

"I'll fix him."

Donna's hands spun the wheel of the car. She guided it into the alley. Bill turned quickly, freezing in the beams of the headlights. His eyes grew wide as Donna came toward him with the car.

"Don't hit him!" Lisa cried.

Donna backed him into the wall. Bill was trapped between the bumper and the concrete foundation of the house. He held up his hands and squinted into the glaring light.

Donna rolled down the window and stuck her head out. "What do you think you're doing back here, Bill Boland?"

"I was coming to see you!" Bill cried.

"Don't lie to me!"

"No, honest," Bill replied. "I have to talk to you, Donna."

"Why?"

"I can't take it anymore," Bill whined. "My conscience . . ."

"What are you talking about?" Donna asked.

"I'm talking about Skip," Bill replied. "I know why he was on Storm Lake when he died."

Bill reached for a glass of soda on the coffee table. He had just finished telling Donna and Lisa about the trick he and Art had pulled on

Skip. He figured that if he was honest about the hazing, Donna and Lisa would never suspect him as the murderer.

Lisa glared at Bill. "You jerk! You fool!"

"Please," Bill said. "That's not all. I think Art had something to do with Skip's death."

Donna frowned at him. "Why?"

"I don't know," Bill replied. "He really didn't like Skip very much. And the whole thing was his idea. I just went along with it because I wanted to have some fun."

"Fun!" Lisa said. "You got Skip killed."

Donna's mother stuck her head into the living room. "Donna, is everything all right?"

"Yes, Mom." Donna looked at Lisa. "Shh."

Lisa glowered at her. "We have to tell the sheriff about this!"

"No!" Bill insisted. "I can't tell the sheriff. I promised Art I wouldn't say a word."

"Then why did you come to us?" Donna asked.

Bill leaned back, the glass of soda trembling in his hand. "I had to tell someone. It's been eating at me."

Lisa stood up. "I'm going to tell."

Donna grabbed her wrist. "No. Please, sit down."

Reluctantly, Lisa eased back onto the couch. "Donna, Skip was on Storm Lake because of that prank Art and Bill played on him."

Donna shook her head. "Like it or not, Skip

went out in that boat of his own free will. Unless we can prove Art did something to cause his death, nobody is going to listen to us."

"That's it," Bill said. "We have to prove that Art did something to Skip. It's the only way."

Lisa exhaled, folding her arms in a gesture of disgust. "I don't like it, Donna. Why should we trust Bill?"

Bill hung his head. "I'm not asking you to forgive me, Lisa. I just want to help you, if I can. I swear it."

"I will never forgive you!" Lisa said in a raspy tone.

She got up and left the room, going into the kitchen.

Donna sighed. "That was a stupid thing you did, Bill."

"I know," he said, looking sad and contrite. "I just want to try to make things right. What do we do now?"

"Well," Donna replied, "the first thing we have to find out is whether or not Skip put that scarf in the basement of the old Bigelow place. If he was in there, it changes everything."

"Somebody could have killed him in the mansion and dragged his body out to the lake," said Bill.

Donna shook her head. "No, I don't think Art killed him. But he might have hazed him on the island. He could have forced Skip out into the water until he was struck by lightning."

"I guess that's possible," said Bill.

"We have to go out there," Donna said. "To the Bigelow estate. That could be tricky this time of year. There aren't many boats left on the water in December. Has the lake started to freeze yet?"

Bill shrugged. "I don't think so."

"I have to get out there, Bill."

He looked into her eyes. "I think I have a way."

Donna leaned back a little. "I'm listening."

"Do you know where Fancy Creek runs into the marsh, on the northwest tip of the lake?" Bill asked.

Donna nodded.

"It's west of the boy scout camp, on the other side of Pine Island," Bill explained. "We could put a boat in there. My father has a twelve-foot inflatable boat with a small motor."

"When can you get it?" Donna asked.

"In a couple of days," Bill replied. "My parents are going to be out of town the day after Christmas."

Donna glanced toward the window. "I hope the lake doesn't ice over by then."

Bill sipped from the glass of soda. His heart was pounding. Sweat had soaked through his clothes. Bill Boland wasn't looking forward to another outing on Storm Lake.

Chapter 16

Art Lawing sat in the living room of his house, staring into a roaring fire. His parents had gone to a pre-Christmas party at the country club. Art was alone for the evening. The solitude made him a little sad.

He stirred a warm cup of apple cider with a cinnamon stick. Donna had always liked mulled cider. They had shared it together many times in front of the fire. Art really missed Donna. It was tough seeing her at the team meetings. She was so cold. Art regretted the way he had treated her, though he would never admit it to anyone.

He sipped at the cider and put the cup back on the coffee table.

He sighed, looking into the fire again. He considered calling Donna, but his pride wouldn't let him. He wouldn't crawl to anyone, not even a beautiful girl like Donna.

"Merry Christmas," he muttered to himself.

Sliding off the sofa, he walked through the shadows of the house. A tall, blue spruce tree had been erected in front of the picture window that faced the lake. Multicolored Christmas lights blinked on and off.

Art went into the kitchen. He was hungry and had decided to make himself a sandwich. He was eating when he finally noticed the square envelope on the door of the refrigerator. It had been stuck there with a magnetic strawberry.

Art put down the sandwich and plucked the envelope from the door. His mother had taped a note beside it: *Art, This got mixed up with my Christmas cards. Sorry. Love, Mom*. He sat down at the butcher-block table where he had been eating.

The envelope was addressed to Art. There was no return address, but the Cresswell postmark had canceled the stamp. It was probably a Christmas card from one of his friends.

He opened the envelope and pulled out the card. The rosy face of Santa Claus looked up at him. Art unfolded the card and looked at the message inside.

His eyes grew wide.

The Yuletide greeting had been covered by a piece of yellow construction paper. Block letters rendered a sentiment that was not exactly in harmony with the joy of the season. Art read it over and over.

RESOLVED: ART LAWING KILLED SKIP. Somebody knew! He hurried to the window upstairs and looked out toward the island. He couldn't see a thing in the darkness. But maybe there was something out there at the Bigelow estate, something that might link him to Skip's death.

He had to go out there. But when? It was too dark, and the lake was rough. There was also slush in the bays, though the water had not frozen yet.

The next couple of days would be tied up with the family get-together, the trappings of Christmas. But he had to go out to Pine Island. He finally decided that he would have to wait until the day after Christmas. Then he would be able to find out what was going on and make sure there was not a shred of evidence to link him to Skip's death.

Chapter 17

The day after Christmas, Donna borrowed her father's car and headed straight for Lisa's house. Lisa was waiting for her on the porch. She ran through the cold air and jumped into the car.

They didn't say a word at first. Donna started out of Cresswell, going through the middle of town. The bell at All Saints' Church rang eight times as they made for the ramp that took them onto the interstate.

"Where's Bill?" Lisa asked.

Donna shrugged. "He said to meet him at Fancy Creek at ten, but I want to get there early."

Lisa folded her arms in disgust. "Merry Christmas," she said in a petulant tone. "What did Santa bring you?"

Donna kept her eyes on the highway. "What's with you?"

"Bill," Lisa replied. "I still don't think we should trust him. He's a real jerk."

Donna sighed. "You might be right, Lisa.

That's one of the reasons I want to get to Fancy Creek a little early. I don't really trust him either, but he did volunteer the information."

"Look," Lisa said, throwing out her hands. "Bill admitted that he and Art made Skip go out on the lake. It was stupid, Donna! Art and Bill should be punished for what they did."

"For daring Skip to do something stupid? Unless one of them did something that directly hurt Skip, there's no way to punish them. We have to have proof, Lisa."

Lisa sighed and looked out the window. "Do you really think they did something to Skip?"

"I don't know," Donna replied. "Bill seems like a puppy dog most of the time. And Art may be arrogant, but I've never known him to even be in a fight. He was never violent toward me. Pushy, but never violent. I don't know if he could hurt someone. As for Jeffrey, he's a dweeb. He *could* be a killer, but—I know this sounds crazy—I just don't think he's got the imagination."

"Bill is the biggest creep," Lisa said. "Always looking at me and smiling. He even called me a couple of times."

"He likes you," Donna offered. "He used to have a crush on me. He was very upset when I started dating Art."

They were quiet for a long time. Donna guided the car down the ramp of the Storm Lake exit. They took the spur road to the road that followed the winding course of the lake-shore.

Along the shore road, the trees were bare and gray. A few evergreens broke up the monotony of the chilly landscape. Suddenly the lake was there, looming around a dark bend. The water was dark and choppy. Some slushy ice had formed near the bank where the snow had drifted. But the lake was still navigable.

Lisa swallowed. "We're here so soon."

Donna nodded. "I know."

They drove for a few more minutes before they saw Pine Island across the deep water. The old Bigelow estate was visible through the fingers of trees. The mansion rested against the clouds on the top of the knoll, unyielding and hostile to all who tried to enter.

Art Lawing stood on the shoreline of Storm Lake with his arms folded over his chest. His eyes were focused on Pine Island across the choppy water. He had burned the piece of yellow construction paper, but the message was still fresh in his mind.

RESOLVED: ART LAWING KILLED SKIP.

The note was meant to scare him. Someone had knowledge of the initiation prank that they had played on Skip. Art had inferred from the message that there was evidence to incriminate him on Pine Island. What if Skip had made it to the island? Art's scarf might still be there if the police hadn't found it. He had to get to Pine Island.

He looked back at the house. His father and mother were still asleep. They were exhausted from the festivities of the day before. Art had not enjoyed his Christmas dinner. He had been preoccupied with the horrible message in the greeting card. He had destroyed the card, burning it and flushing the ashes down the toilet, not wanting his parents to find it and question his involvement in Skip's death.

Turning toward the boathouse, Art stepped carefully in the thin layer of snow. He was dressed in a ski suit. Beneath the suit, he wore a diving garment that had been designed for cold temperatures. He wanted to stay warm on the water. His father's boat was in storage, but he had a kayak stashed in the shed.

Art pulled the kayak to the water's edge. He went back for the paddle and a life jacket. A ski mask covered his face. For a moment he imagined himself on a secret mission to save the world. But he was only trying to save himself.

After easing the kayak into the water, he pulled it to the side of the dock. He slid down into the craft, through the rubber ring that fit tightly around his midsection. The ring kept water from splashing into the boat.

Using the double paddle, he pushed himself away from the dock. He dug both sides of the paddle into the water. The waves lapped over the tip of the kayak. Art guided it back toward shore, finding a calm seam along the bank. With the paddle working, he was able to pick up speed.

Art could follow the bays and inlets of the western shore until he reached Loon Point. The point formed a windbreak. From there, he could make a straight shot across the lake to Pine Island and the Bigelow estate.

Fancy Creek ran through a private plot of land that had been used for years as a park by the locals. The owner didn't mind sharing access to the lake as long as everyone treated the land with respect. Donna turned onto an unmarked road that led back into the forest.

The bare trees rose up on both sides of the dirt road. High clouds covered the morning sun, rendering fingery shadows on the hood of the car. Donna drove slowly, guiding the car through the lonely woods.

The road widened into a clearing beside the creek. Beyond the cleared area, they could see the straw-colored marshes of a swampland called Smoky Bog. It was the only backwater of Storm Lake.

Lisa squinted at the bog. "Creepy."

"Yes," Donna replied, "but at least we got here before Bill. Come on, let's have a look around."

They climbed out and started toward the dark, forbidding waters of Fancy Creek.

Bill Boland was desperately late for his appointment with Donna and Lisa. All morning he had been preparing for the journey. The boat and motor had barely fit into the trunk of his car.

He had to do it. There was no other way. His head could not take the pounding much longer. He had to relieve himself of the burden.

After climbing into his new car, Bill turned the ignition key. The engine whirred for more than a minute but refused to come to life. He tried again, but the engine lost energy and became flooded. He slammed the steering wheel with his palm. Now what was he going to do?

"I bet Bill doesn't even show up," Lisa said. "This is another one of his stupid stunts."

Donna was staring at the creek. It flowed along a path that led down to Storm Lake. She had been on the trail along the creek many times when she was growing up in Cresswell. But she had never felt so threatened by the shadows of the woods that surrounded the path.

"Let's go," Lisa said. "Bill's not coming. It's already ten after ten. He was just talking. He wanted to impress me so I'd go out with him."

Donna pointed toward the path. "I want to walk down to the lake."

Lisa shivered. "Why?"

"Because. I just want to."

Lisa didn't want to be alone in the clearing. "I'll come with you."

They started down the narrow trail. The woods were silent. Their footsteps were not enough to disturb the eerie calm. Just before they reached the lake, they passed an overturned rowboat that was covered by a canvas tarp. Someone had either forgotten about the aluminum vessel or had left it there for use during the winter.

They emerged from the woods at the shoreline of Storm Lake. Waves lapped against the rocks, but it was not too choppy. Donna looked out toward Pine Island. Her eyes grew wide. She thought she saw someone in a small boat, making for the cove at the base of the Bigelow estate.

When Art pushed the kayak beyond the shelter of Indian Point, the lake waters grew rough around him. He took a deep breath. He felt strong. Adrenaline was coursing through his veins. The cold hadn't affected him yet, but he was going to be swamped in the whitecaps if he didn't concentrate on maintaining control of the kayak. Storm Lake was threatening to swallow him whole.

He started to work the paddle harder. The kayak went forward in a depression between the rolling waves. It did not seem any worse than the rapids he had experienced in Canada on his last vacation. He managed to navigate the troughs and crests of the chop, making headway toward the forlorn mound of Pine Island. The kayak slipped through the rough water, slicing toward the cove where Skip had taken the canoe ashore just three months ago.

Art could see the rocks at the mouth of the cove. The vessel shot past the rocks. He was inside the cove. The water flattened out immediately. Art paddled until the nose bumped against the rocky shoreline.

He lifted the paddle over his head. "Yeah!"

Climbing out, he caught a glimpse of the snowy backdrop on the incline above him. He skipped a breath. He could also see the dark shape on top of the hill, half hidden behind the evergreens. The old Bigelow place seemed to be glaring down at him.

Art hadn't forgotten why he had come. The kayak trip suddenly seemed worth the trouble. If there was evidence in the old mansion, at least Art was in a position to recover it. Even if he was afraid, he had to follow through with his plan.

Art shivered. The air suddenly felt colder. He knew what he had to do. He couldn't listen to the fearful little voice that told him to turn back. His heart pounded as his eyes studied the path that rose toward the dilapidated mansion. After a few moments, he began to climb the granite steps, all the while thinking of Cresswell scarves and of heads that had never been found.

Lisa watched as Donna uncovered the aluminum rowboat that sat back in the bare trees. "Here, Donna, let me give you a hand."

They threw back the tarp that had been covering the abandoned vessel. The dinghy was only ten feet long. The narrow beam was not suited to the turbulent surface of Storm Lake.

Donna sighed. "I hope we can make it out to Pine Island in this thing."

Lisa nodded. "It's crazy, but I know we have to try. Do you really think we're going to find something out there?"

Donna glanced at her friend. "Who knows? At least we have to give it a try, if only for our own peace of mind."

"I think there's something out there Bill doesn't want us to find," said Lisa. "He's too embarrassed to face us. That's why he didn't show up."

"Unless he already went out to Pine Island to rearrange the evidence," Donna suggested, thinking of the figure she had just seen in the distance. "At least that gives us a chance to have a look for ourselves. Come on, let's get this thing in the water."

They flipped the dinghy on its hull and found two flimsy, wooden oars wedged beneath the seats. There were no life jackets to go along with the oars.

Lisa looked at Donna. "We have to do it, don't we?"

Donna nodded. "There's no other way. I want to sink Bill. I know he's got something to do with all this."

Lisa's expression became grim. "Donna, what if Art is somehow involved in this?"

"I've thought of that," Donna said as they finally managed to ease the dinghy into the water. "But if we think about it too much, we might decide not to go."

The dinghy was fairly stable as it bobbed in the mouth of Fancy Creek. Donna climbed in and put the oars in the oarlocks.

Lisa also boarded the fragile craft. She sat in the stern.

Donna's gloved hands gripped the handles of the oars. "Here goes nothing," she said under her breath.

Midway up the hill, Art stopped to peer toward the gray mansion. Clouds hung low over the island, deepening the shroud around the shadowy estate. Art's breath fogged the chilly air through the hole in the ski mask. He felt an urge to turn back. But he had already decided to get in and out as quickly as possible.

Resuming the climb, Art took each step slowly. He had been to the Bigelow estate many times, but he had never felt such fear slicing through his guts. What if someone was drawing him into a trap? What if Skip had come back from the dead to claim his revenge?

As he ascended the last tier, he hesitated, looking toward the mansion. For a moment, Art thought he saw a head in a piece of broken window. But when he looked again, it seemed to have been only the reflection of a cloud in the glass. The window was empty except for the darkness behind it.

Art remembered the message. Who had sent him the bizarre Christmas card? Maybe it was a practical joke of Bill's. Perhaps Bill had knowledge of something Skip left behind on the island. Why wouldn't Bill tell him directly? He could have called or mentioned something at the debating-team meeting. Maybe he had discovered the information during the vacation.

The wind blew around his shoulders. His winter garments wouldn't stave off the chill that came from within. He began to move again, heading for the front steps of the house. The entire structure seemed to be shifting and creaking in the stiff, frigid breeze.

"I'm out of my mind," he muttered to himself.

He ascended the rickety steps and peered through the open door. He tried to recall the layout of the old house from his previous explorations. He flinched when a strange noise echoed from the bowels of the mansion. He thought he had heard a footstep.

"Who's there!"

The whistling wind was his only reply. Art tried to swallow. His mouth had gotten dry. A burning sensation throbbed in his chest. His fate hung on what he could find inside the house. He had to give it a shot.

Striding boldly through the front door, Art looked straight ahead. He could see that the basement door was open at the end of the hallway. He peered into the shadows of the stairwell, wishing he had brought a flashlight. Slowly and gingerly, he began his descent. Halfway down, he was able to scan the rafters, but there was no sign of a scarf. He turned to start up the basement stairs.

Art froze when he heard a bump in another part of the house. It was a clear, loud nose. There was somebody else in the house! He waited, while his heart ricocheted in his chest. Then he heard heavy, plodding footsteps coming from one of the upper floors. It wasn't the wind.

Grabbing a loose piece of timber from the hallway, Art started up the steps to the second floor. His body tingled with the anticipation of discovery. He had to find out who had summoned him to the Bigelow estate.

A few steps from the second-floor landing, he heard his name being called in a cold, electronic voice. "Art. Art Lawing."

The voice had come from above. It sounded a lot like the voice that Art and Bill had used on Skip.

"Bill? Are you up there?"

The voice echoed again. "Art. Art Lawing."

"Boland," Art said bravely, "I know that's you."

More footsteps sounded.

Art was scared. This wasn't a joke any longer.

"Hey, Boland, old buddy. You don't have to do this. We're a team, remember? We promised to stick together. You hear me? We can work this out."

Art continued to climb the creaking staircase. When he reached the top, he paused, listening for more footfalls. The only sound was the whistling of the cold wind. Art stepped up to the first empty room, glancing into the bare shadows. There was no sign of Bill Boland.

"Hey, Bill, old pal. Let's get together on this. We made it this far. Why not hash it out like old buddies?"

No reply. Art kept moving in the hallway, glancing into one empty room after another. If he had looked to his left, he would have seen the girls, struggling across the lake in a dinghy,

127

framed in the dusty window. But his eyes were trained forward, anticipating another surprise.

His throat was dry as he called out, "Bill, I know it's you. You don't have to play this with me. We can talk. Hey, we've been buddies a long time. Be a friend."

When he reached the end of the hallway, Art found a set of steps that led up to the third floor. Something clumped overhead. Art felt his stomach turning. Bill was probably waiting for him with a fright mask and a whooping cry.

"Bill, you better come down!" he hollered.

But the clumping had stopped. The wind shook the rafters as Art began his climb to the third floor. He emerged slowly into the third-floor hallway. There was a bare room to his right. Light streaked in through a hole in the ceiling, illuminating the attic apartment.

"You're trying to yank my chain, Boland," Art said with mock bravado. "I don't like it."

He looked around frantically. Nobody was there. The place was empty except for something that hung suspended from the ceiling. Art lost his breath when he saw his Cresswell scarf, the same one he had given to Skip. The scarf seemed to be floating in midair.

Art had to get the scarf and clear out in a hurry. He would take care of Bill later. For now, he had to grab the evidence and paddle the kayak back across the lake.

As he drew closer to the scarf, he saw that it

dangled from the end of a thin wire. It swayed over a hole in the floor. A single board spanned the gaping hole, which must have been eight feet across. Art could see the second floor beneath him. He reached for the scarf, but it was not within his grasp. If he wanted the scarf, he would have to step out onto the board to get it.

Putting one foot on the board, he fought for his balance. He hoped his years of skiing would help him now. He was able to dart out over the hole in a few easy steps. His hand closed around the dangling scarf.

"Yeah!" Art said triumphantly.

But suddenly something had fallen over Art's head. He felt the rope tightening around his neck. His fingers groped at the noose, trying to rip it from his throat, but it was too late. He teetered on the board, desperately trying to free himself and keep his balance.

But the board fell out from beneath his feet. As he tumbled through the hole in the floor, the soft flesh of his stomach caught on a jagged, protruding nail. The rusty point ripped across him, opening his torso.

Art hung from the ceiling with his entrails pouring onto the floor below.

He kicked and flailed helplessly as the life flowed from his body.

"Look," Lisa cried. "We're almost there!"

Pine Island loomed in front of them. When

the dinghy hit the beach, they jumped from the boat.

Lisa glanced back over her shoulder when the craft was secure. "We can follow the shoreline until we find a path up to the house."

Donna nodded. They began to step carefully along the rocky bank. It felt good to be moving. When they rounded a stony curve on the shore, they jumped to the top of a large boulder. From the rocks, they could see the kayak in the cove.

"Where did that come from?" Lisa asked.

"It belongs to Art," Donna replied. "I recognize it. He keeps it in the boathouse."

Lisa glanced upward, looking at the mansion on the hill. "Why is Art up there, Donna?"

"Let's go find out."

They jumped down on the other side of the boulder. Walking around the cove, they passed the kayak. Donna stopped at the bottom of the path that led toward the summit of the snowy hill. Lisa stood beside her. They both peered up at the mansion.

Then the dark-haired girl pushed past Donna, taking the lead. She started up the tiers of granite steps. Donna came after her.

When they reached the top of the hill, they stopped, gazing at the dark house. They looked at each other, nodded, and continued toward the steps of the old mansion. The truth was waiting for them inside.

As soon as they were inside, they began poking around downstairs. Then they started for the second floor. Lisa led the way. She crept down the cold, dusty hallway, peeking into each room. When she saw the pool of blood on the floor and the feet dangling through the hole in the ceiling overhead, she screamed.

Donna raced up to her. Together they stood transfixed in the doorway, staring at the body hanging from the third-floor rafters. Donna had to step right up to the pool of blood and entrails and look up through the ceiling to see that it was Art hanging there, turning back and forth in the drafts of chilly air.

Only then did both girls notice the writing on the far wall, huge letters that had been scrawled in red spray paint.

I LOST DONNA. I KILLED SKIP. GOOD-BYE.

Chapter 18

A cold, harsh January wind swept over Cresswell, bringing the brittle hand of deep winter to the valley. Art Lawing's funeral would be delayed by the investigation into his death. He was going to be buried the day after New Year's, but the coroner's report put back the ceremony another week.

The sheriff had grilled Donna and Lisa several times before he pronounced the case closed. The local authorities were satisfied that Art had committed suicide over his guilt about killing Skip. Donna and Lisa were not so convinced.

Donna drove Lisa to the cemetery for the funeral. It was the same graveyard where Skip was buried. The two grieving girls trudged across the icy ground, moving toward the tiny gathering. Art's parents, a few relatives, and the pastor were the only ones there besides Donna and Lisa. No one from Cresswell High wanted to attend the funeral of a murderer.

The two girls hung back a bit, not sure they

would be welcomed by the Lawings. Art's mother turned to look at them. Donna nodded at her. Tears welled in Lisa's eyes as the words were spoken over the coffin.

After Art's body was lowered into the grave, Mrs. Lawing came toward the girls. Donna held her breath, wondering what to say on such a sad occasion. Mrs. Lawing extended her hands to Donna.

Donna embraced her. "I'm so sorry, Mrs. Lawing. I'm so sorry."

"Thank you for coming, Donna. It means a lot to me. I . . ." Her voice cracked.

Donna stepped back a little. "Mrs. Lawing, I don't think Art could have done what they said."

Mrs. Lawing shook her head. "It's over, Donna. I . . ." She could not finish the sentence. She moved away, joining her distraught husband.

Lisa put her hand on Donna's shoulder. "Maybe we'd better go."

Donna sighed. "I still can't believe Art killed Skip. Art was a lot of things, but he wasn't a murderer, Lisa. He couldn't kill someone. I knew him better than anyone. He was arrogant, petty, jealous. But he wasn't evil."

Lisa nodded. "But we don't have any proof that Art was innocent."

"Bill Boland," Donna replied coldly. "He's

the one who was supposed to meet us. But he never showed up. Why?"

"He said his car broke down," Lisa replied.

"I don't trust him," Donna went on. "Bill is too sneaky. You said he was creepy."

"I know, I know."

Donna and Lisa looked toward the grave. They had told the sheriff about Bill's involvement in their trip to the Bigelow estate. The sheriff had interrogated Bill, but he had been released. Bill seemed above suspicion, except for the girls' doubts about him.

"Come on, Donna. Let's go. We've got school tomorrow. Mr. Ferris wants to have a meeting of the debate team."

"All right."

They walked back to the car. Donna sat behind the wheel, staring straight ahead until Lisa urged her to start the engine. They headed back toward Cresswell, unaware of the eyes that marked their departure from the cemetery.

Bill Boland had parked on the cemetery grounds and had watched Art Lawing's funeral from his car. He had lucked out on Art's suicide, although he thought it strange that someone with such a big ego would do himself in. He knew Donna had suspicions about his involvement in Skip's death. And he felt it was too bad that the girls had not been killed when they were on the island. Donna was smart and resourceful enough to stay on his trail, and that worried him.

Bill followed Donna and Lisa back to Cresswell, all the time thinking about the way he had handled the sheriff. Bill had come clean about Skip's initiation prank, pleading that he had just been one of the guys. He also told the authorities that he had been suspicious of Art all along. He had planned the trip to the lake with the girls to spy on Art. He didn't tell the sheriff that he was luring the girls to the island so he could kill them.

Art was dead, and Skip was dead. Bill was in the clear. Nothing pointed to him as Skip's killer. For the time being, his headaches had stopped.

He guided his car past Donna's house, wondering if she might cause trouble for him. He hated Donna for turning Lisa against him. Donna might have to be dealt with eventually. Bill would have to play it cool.

He had no idea that the headaches would start again after the debate-team meeting the next day.

Chapter 19

Mr. Ferris had resolved to keep the debating team alive. Bill, Donna, and Jeffrey were now the core of the team. But there were also plans to hold more tryouts for new members. The team would be weaker without Art and Skip, but they were not going under.

At the meeting that afternoon, Mr. Ferris told his team that the scholarship would now be called the Skip Masters Endowment. He also explained his new strategy for the coming spring debates.

As Mr. Ferris spoke, Bill leaned back with his cheek in his hand. He felt Donna's eyes on him. He had detected a strange glint in Donna's eyes. Maybe she knew he had murdered Skip. It was obvious in her manner. Lisa also gave him dirty looks as she passed him in the hall. They both knew!

"Bill?"

He looked up from his daydreaming. Mr. Ferris was staring at him. Donna also glared in his direction. Bill had not heard a word of Mr. Ferris's speech.

"I'm sorry," Bill said awkwardly. "I'm out of it today."

"It's all right," Mr. Ferris said in a sympathetic tone. "We've all been through a rough time. But we'll make it."

The bell rang to end the meeting. Bill got up and left in a rush without looking at Donna. He hurried to his locker, swinging it open. Something fluttered to his feet. He unfolded the yellow construction paper. The same block letters jumped out at him. RESOLVED: YOU'RE DEAD!

His head started to pound again.

"Donna," Bill muttered to himself. "That hateful—"

A hand fell on his shoulder. Bill turned to see Jeffrey Goodman standing there. Bill's face was ashen.

"Hey, are you all right?" Jeffrey asked.

"No," Bill replied. "Look at this."

He showed Jeffrey the piece of paper. Jeffrey's eyes grew wide as he read the words. He quickly folded up the paper and gave it back to Bill.

"What's going on?" Jeffrey asked.

Bill eyed him carefully. Something had snapped inside Bill. He knew he had to kill Donna and Lisa before they squealed on him. And he thought Jeffrey might be able to help.

"Meet me tonight," Bill said. "Unless you're chicken."

"Sure," Jeffrey replied softly. "I'll meet you. I want to hear all about it."

That evening Bill paced back and forth in his room, talking to Jeffrey. "It's Donna, that witch. She's after me. She thinks I had something to do with Skip's death. Everybody knows Art killed him."

Jeffrey frowned at Bill. "You were in on the prank with Skip."

"Yes, but I didn't kill him! I swear. Now Donna is going after me. She left me that note."

Jeffrey shook his head. "Man, she's flipped out if she's trying to terrorize you."

"Lisa is in on it, too," Bill replied. "I know it."

Bill looked sideways at Jeffrey to see if Jeffrey was buying the act. It would be great if he could talk Jeffrey into helping him do away with Donna and Lisa. Of course, that might mean getting rid of Jeffrey, too.

"I can't take it anymore," Bill whined.

Jeffrey sighed. "You know, I never liked those two girls."

"What can I do?" Bill asked.

"Keep an eye on them," Jeffrey replied.

"Jeffrey, I think Donna might have killed Art."

"If that's true," Jeffrey replied, "then we can

sink her in the water. She might be planning to frame you, Bill. If she does that, then Donna Forsi is definitely on thin ice."

Donna sat at the computer terminal, calling up notes for the debate team. But her mind wasn't on her work. Her thoughts turned constantly to the image of Art swinging from a rope in the Bigelow mansion. She was positive that Art couldn't have killed himself or Skip. But two weeks had passed, and she still didn't have any proof.

Donna absently put in the code for the computer file that she needed. She punched in the wrong number. An unexpected classification flashed across the screen. *Skip's Death: Art Lawing.*

Her heart skipped a beat. She began to access the file, reading the words that came up on the screen. She couldn't believe it. Art had been trying to find out what had really happened to Skip. He wanted to get Skip's death off his conscience. He had been using a secret file in the computer to store his notes.

"Donna?"

She almost jumped out of her chair. Lisa had come in behind her. They had planned to meet in the computer room after school.

"Lisa, look at this."

Lisa's eyes bulged as she read. "My Lord, Art

140

didn't kill Skip at all. We've got to take this to the sheriff."

"No! The sheriff is not about to believe something like this. Not just yet, at least."

Lisa shivered. "Donna, what are we going to do?"

Donna sighed. "There's only one thing we can do," she replied. "We have to go back to Pine Island and see if we can find some more evidence."

"Pine Island," Lisa said with a shudder. But she knew it was the right thing to do.

Bill watched as Donna and Lisa entered the parking lot of Cresswell High. He followed them across the parking lot for a few minutes and then went back to his car. He knew Donna was going home, so he took a shortcut and ended up down the street from her house.

Donna arrived with Lisa, and they both went into the house. He waited five minutes until they came out again. They went behind the house and emerged from the alley in Donna's father's car.

Bill followed them again until they hit the interstate. His heart began to pound. He pulled off and stopped at a pay phone. His fingers fumbled with the coin, then shoved it into the slot. He dialed quickly.

"Jeffrey, it's me, Bill. It's on. Yeah, they're

heading out that way. Where? Storm Lake, man. I think they're going to Pine Island."

Donna parked the car on the northeastern shore of the frozen lake. A path through the bare woods took her and Lisa to edge of the ice. She had chosen the northeastern shore because the ice near Fancy Creek was too thin for walking. Every year or so, a fisherman's shanty fell through the ice there. They had to cross the lake where the ice was thick.

As the girls stared across the lake at the darkening mound of Pine Island, they heard the low whine of a snowmobile somewhere in the distance. They were both frightened of their task, but they had to do it. This was just the beginning of the investigation. Art would be vindicated if they were right.

"You know," Donna said, "there were no suicide warning signs from Art. Not one."

Lisa nodded. "What if we don't find anything over there?"

"Then we keep looking," Donna replied. "If worse comes to worst, we can take that computer file to the sheriff."

"Sure."

"Come on," Donna said. "Let's go."

They started across the frozen surface of the lake. The ice was thick enough to hold their weight. By the time they reached the island, it was dusk. They were warm from their exertions, so they took off their jackets and hid them in some bushes.

Their legs were aching by the time they reached the mansion. As they moved cautiously toward the steps, they could see the open maw of the house gaping at them, daring them to enter. They moved slowly up the walk, climbing the steps. A blast of frigid air rushed over them as they passed through the doorway.

"This is creepy," Lisa said.

Donna nodded. "We better hurry before all the light is—"

Something clumped on the second floor of the house.

"Somebody's up there, Donna."

"I'm going to find out who it is."

"I'm going with you," Lisa replied.

They mounted the stairs, heading for the room where Art had died. In the last dim light of the afternoon, they peered toward the red spray paint that had not been erased. Underneath the message, painted in black, were the words *Resolved: You're dead!* Donna moved closer to study the writing.

As she stepped away, Lisa screamed suddenly. Donna turned back to see that someone had grabbed Lisa from behind. The intruder, wearing a stocking mask, had put a knife to her throat.

"Now stay really still or I cut off her head," a male voice said.

Donna recognized the voice immediately. "Bill Boland!"

"That's right, babe. Ole Bill. The guy you never liked." He pulled off the stocking mask.

Donna glared at him. "*You* killed Skip!"

"Yes, and now I'm going to kill both of you."

Donna didn't move. "You can't get away with it, Bill. Somebody will find you out."

"I've gotten away with it so far," Bill replied. "You stupid girls. All you had to do was love me. Either one of you. But no. I wasn't good enough for you. You had to go for the rich kid and the hotshot sophomore."

"You're sick," Lisa cried. "I could never love you."

"You killed Art, too," Donna accused. "You lured him up here and put a rope around his neck. He was onto you, Bill. I found the computer file."

"Shut up!" Bill cried. "I didn't kill Art. He was my friend. We swore we wouldn't tell anyone about Skip. I—yoww—"

Bill's eyes grew wide all of a sudden. He gave a hollow grunt, letting go of Lisa. The knife dropped from his hand. Lisa ran to Donna, looking back as Bill slumped to the floor with a boning knife protruding from his back. Someone moved through the shadowed doorway. Bill twitched on the floor, fighting for breath. The intruder stood over him, looking down at the body.

144

"Jeffrey!" Lisa cried. "Thank God. You saved us."

Donna gazed toward Jeffrey Goodman. "How did you know we were out here?"

"Bill told me," Jeffrey replied.

Donna started to take a step toward him, but Jeffrey raised a pistol, pointing it at them. "Don't move, girls. We aren't finished yet."

Donna gaped at the pistol. "What are you doing?"

Jeffrey grinned. "You might as well know the truth, since you're going to be dead soon. I killed Art. I pulled off the suicide number. Now I'm going to kill both of you and frame Bill for it."

Lisa glared at him. "*You* killed Skip!"

Jeffrey shook his head. "No. I only killed Art. Bill did in Skip so he could have a shot at you. Stupid, isn't it? Killing someone over a woman."

"Why?" Donna asked. "Why did you kill Art?"

"He was in my way," Jeffrey replied. "If I had let him live, he would have won the scholarship. Ten thousand dollars is a good reason to kill someone. That's why I have to kill you, Donna. I want all the competition erased."

"You monster!" Lisa cried.

"No, I'm a genius," Jeffrey went on. "Everyone will be gone, and I'll have the scholarship. It'll seem like Bill lost it and killed both of you.

I'll have to make it look good, but I can pull it off the same way I killed Art. I figured Bill had killed Skip all along, but I wasn't sure. So I sent him little notes. I sent the same notes to Art. I figured one of them would come back out here. I never dreamed I'd be lucky enough to catch Art all alone. But I pulled it off. Imagine how I'll be a hero when I say I tried to save both of you. I was just a little bit late. Now, if I can just get this body in the right position . . ."

As he bent toward Bill's corpse, Donna saw her chance. She rushed him, knocking Jeffrey to the floor. Lisa was right behind her, running for the stairs. They heard the gun explode, but Jeffrey missed them. They made it into the living room as he fired again. The slug slammed into the wall above them. Plaster rained down on their heads.

They ran through the house, and out onto the stoop. They had to take the path down in the growing darkness. A burning sensation filled their chests as they breathed in the frigid air. But they couldn't stop. As they made it into the woods surrounding the mansion, four more shots nipped through the branches around them.

They made it to the ice unscathed. Donna looked behind her. Jeffrey was nowhere in sight.

"Lisa, let's go."

They were halfway across the lake when

they heard the sound of the whining engine. They hesitated, looking back as the whine of the motor drew closer. Two beady headlights came straight at them.

"What is it?" Lisa cried.

"My God," Donna said. "He's got a snowmobile. He must've used it to get to the island before us."

"No. He'll catch us for sure."

Donna turned to her right. "We've got to run away from the car. That's the first place he'll look. There."

They began to stumble toward the marsh and Fancy Creek. Donna knew they would never be able to outdistance the snowmobile. They had to change directions, to confuse Jeffrey. If they could get to the highway before he caught them, they might be able to help.

They could hear the noise of the motor getting closer. Donna looked back to see the lights circling toward them.

Lisa dropped to one knee. "Can't go on."

"Come on," Donna gasped. "We can't give up now."

They tried to sprint, but their bodies were too tired. They would never be able to get off the frozen lake before the snowmobile overtook them.

From behind, they could hear his high-pitched maniacal laugh. "Nice try, Forsi. Too bad it didn't work. The debate team is going to miss you. They'll probably add your name to the scholarship when I frame Boland for killing you."

Donna gulped air, trying to stall for time. "You'll never get away with it, Jeffrey."

"Sure I will."

He was five or six yards away from them, sitting in the seat of the snowmobile. He held the gun in his hand. She knew that, unless he had put a new clip in the gun, it was out of bullets. Donna considered rushing at him.

Jeffrey continued to drag it out, savoring the moment of his triumph. "With you out of the way, Forsi, I'll be in line for that scholarship. Ten thousand big ones. I can see it in the paper now. They'll say how I tried to save you from Bill. Of course, I'll say how I managed to kill him in the struggle, but not before he shot both of you."

"Leave us alone!" Donna cried.

Jeffrey leaned back and laughed.

Donna heard the cracking sound in the sheet of ice. Apparently Jeffrey had heard it, too. The ice was giving way under the weight of the snowmobile. Suddenly Jeffrey stopped laughing and tried to climb off, but it was too late.

His voice rose in a pitiful wailing. "Noooo . . ."

The snowmobile crashed through the ice, sinking Jeffrey into the cold water. The girls could hear him splashing and crying out as his voice grew weaker.

They tried to step toward Jeffrey, but the ice cracked again under their feet. A giant crevice had opened in the frozen surface. The freezing water was swallowing Jeffrey. They had to jump back before the lake claimed them, too. The splitting ice drove them back toward shore. By the time they were thirty feet away, they could no longer hear Jeffrey splashing.

"He's gone," Lisa said in a low voice.

"We better go call the sheriff."

Later that evening, when they returned to the ice hole with the deputies, Jeffrey's body was floating facedown in the water. They watched as the deputies fished his corpse from the lake. The deputies questioned them for a long time after they found Bill dead in the old Bigelow mansion. Even then, the sheriff's men weren't sure they could believe the improbable story.

Chapter 20

The warm spring weather had finally lifted the veil of winter from the valley. Summer vacation was only a week away, which meant that Cresswell High was holding its annual awards ceremony during fifth period. The entire student body had gathered in the gymnasium for the event. Donna and Lisa sat together in the bleachers, watching as the awards were given for academic and athletic excellence.

"You're going to win the debating scholarship," Lisa told Donna.

Donna shrugged. "Maybe. If they even decide to give the scholarship this year. Our team didn't do too well in the spring debates."

The "team" had consisted of Donna, one smart but erratic junior, and two green sophomores. Their record in competition had been one victory and four losses. Mr. Ferris had been happy with the single victory, since he had expected the team to lose every contest. He had also been pleased when Lisa returned to serve as the team's secretary.

Donna leaned back a little in her seat. She felt mixed emotions about the end of the school year. Like Lisa, she had recovered from the horrors that had taken place on Pine Island. But the emptiness still swept over her sometimes, threatening to swallow her like the hole in the ice that had claimed Jeffrey Goodman.

The demolition of the old Bigelow estate had made her happy. A developer had plans to build summer homes on the island. Many citizens of Cresswell had wondered aloud if the head of Mrs. Bigelow would turn up during the excavations of the mansion's foundation. So far the construction workers had not found anything resembling a skull. Donna shuddered at the thought.

"Here," Lisa said. "This is it."

Mr. Ferris stepped up to the microphone on the gym floor. "Good afternoon. As you all know, the debating team suffered many setbacks this year. I don't want to dwell on our misfortunes, except to say that the ten-thousand-dollar scholarship for debating excellence is now called the Masters/Lawing Endowment. Please observe a moment of silence for our departed orators."

When the moment of silence was over, the student body erupted into applause, a show of respect for Skip and Art. Art's last name had been added to the scholarship after the authorities learned the truth about his death. The mention of their names brought tears to the eyes of Donna and Lisa. Donna reached into her purse for a tissue. She gave one to Lisa as well.

Mr. Ferris went on with his speech. "So it gives me great pleasure to announce the winner of the Masters/Lawing award for debating excellence. The ten thousand dollars goes to the anchor of our spring debates, Miss Donna Forsi!"

Applause rose in the gym as Donna walked down to accept the check. Mr. Ferris asked her to say a few words. Donna fought back tears as she stood in front of the microphone.

"This award means a lot to me," Donna said. "If Art and Skip were still here, I probably would not have won the scholarship. I'd like to share the money with Art and Skip, but since they're no longer with us, I'd like to share it with someone else. Lisa Enright, I know you're only a sophomore, but come down here and take half this award."

Lisa was stunned. She walked slowly out of the bleachers as the student body gave her a standing ovation. She hugged Donna in front of the microphone. But when Mr. Ferris asked her to say something, she was crying too hard to find the words.